The Trial of Sören Qvist

Janet Lewis

Robin Clark Ltd
London

First published in Great Britain in 1986 by
Robin Clark Ltd
A member of the Namara Group
27/29 Goodge Street, London W1P 1FD

First published in the United States of America
by The Swallow Press Incorporated
1139 South Wabash Avenue
Chicago, Illinois 60605

British Library Cataloguing in Publication Data
Lewis, Janet
The trial of Sören Qvist.
I. Title
813'.52[F]   PS3523.E866
ISBN 0-86072-107-8

Reproduced, printed and bound in Great Britain by
Hazell Watson & Viney Limited,
Member of the BPCC Group,
Aylesbury, Bucks

TO
MACLIN GUÉRARD

Foreword

The story of the Parson of Vejlby is famous in Denmark. Steen Steesen Blicher (1782–1848), himself a Jutlander and a Parson, tells it in his Knitting Room Stories.

I first came across it myself in a volume by Phillips called Famous Cases of Circumstantial Evidence. The only date I have been able to find for Phillips is the year 1814, when "Chief Baron Gilbert was superseded as an authority on the English laws of evidence by the books of Phillips." He may have found his account in the story by Blicher, although I think, from certain differences of detail, that he had another source, possibly the same one Blicher had. At all events, I am sure that the story of Sören Jensen Qvist is, in its main facts and in many of its details, and even in some of the speeches of important characters, history rather than fiction. It would be impossible as well as foolish to attempt an archeologically correct version of the legend. However, I believe that there is nothing in my account of the Parson of Vejlby which might not have happened as I tell it. He is one of a great company of men and women who have preferred to lose their lives rather than accept a universe without plan or without meaning.

There was said to be, before the presence of the Germans in Denmark, the cross in Aalsö churchyard which the Parson of Aalsö raised to the memory of his friend. I trust that it is still there.

APRIL 11, 1946

The Trial of Sören Qvist

Chapter 1

The inn lay in a hollow, the low hill, wooded with leafless beech trees, rising behind it in a gentle round just high enough to break the good draft from the inn chimneys, so that on this chill day the smoke rose a little and then fell downward. The air was clouded with dampness. It was late November, late in the afternoon, but no sunlight came from the west, and to the east the sky was walled with cloud where the cold fog thickened above the shores of Jutland. There was a smell of sea in the air even these few miles inland, but the foot traveler who had come upon sight of the inn had been so close to the sea for so many days now that he was unaware of the salty fragrance.

The inn was familiar to him, and he thought he remembered what lay beyond the turn of the road as it circled the wooded hill and disappeared in shadow. Something in the aspect of the inn was also unfamiliar to him as he stood looking down at it from his side of the hollow where it lay shrouded in its own exhalations. The sign of the Golden Lion still hung above the door, although much of the fine bright yellow paint was gone from the wood. The last pale flakes were in tone now like the beech leaves which clung to the saplings at the edge of the denuded forest. When he had last seen it, the paint had been as fresh as buttercups. That was in the heyday of the king's loves, when the inn had been named in honor of the king's bastard children, all Golden Lions, the illegitimate children of the king being still more noble than the legitimate children of most people. Now that the king was old, and Denmark shrunken and impoverished by his reign, some of the Golden Lions had indeed shown themselves most noble. Others were quarreling among themselves. But here even in Jutland, which had suffered most from the King's wars, the reign of Christian the Fourth was still considered glorious. Even the wayfarer looking down upon the Golden Lion, when he thought of the King, thought of him as splendid. Failing in health, blind in one eye ever since the great naval battle of the Kolberger Heide, and now turned sixtynine, Christian was, in this year of 1646, even more the hero of his people than in his lusty and extravagant youth.

But there was more than loss of paint from the sign to change the appearance of the inn. The traveler had remembered it with an open door, light streaming out generously upon the road before it, and with people coming and going. This evening the door was closed and all the windows were shuttered. There was no one in sight. Something about the shape of the inn seemed changed, as well, but after slow searching in his memory the traveler concluded that it was not the inn itself, but its background and setting, that had suffered loss. Surely he could remember a small wooden dwelling just beyond the innyard, and another across the road from it, but these were gone now. The inn was no longer one of a group, but solitary.

This matter of closed doors and shuttered windows was not new to him since he had first entered the outlying districts of Jutland. He had come through inhospitable and half-deserted country. He had passed farms but poorly under cultivation, and farmhouses still unroofed in which the thick grass of Jutland grew above charred timbers fallen into the dwelling rooms. But he had somehow taken it for granted, in his slow mind, that when he reached his own county and his own parish, things would be as they had been, the doors open and the people kindly.

He went down the slight hill, limping, because the heel was gone from one boot, and the sole of the other had loosened, letting enter the sand and fine gravel. He approached the inn, and knocked. The Golden Lion hung above his head without creaking, so still and heavy was the air. A fawn-colored hound with a tail as long as a whip crept round the corner of the building and stared at him suspiciously with pale yellow eyes, then, hearing the door start open, turned and ran, the long tail curled under its belly. A young woman with a good tall figure, a firm bosom and straight shoulders, came out of the inn and closed the door behind her, holding one hand still upon the latch.

With her came the aroma of the inn. It clung to the

heavy serge of her garments, and she stood before the stranger in a sensuous aureole of warm air. The smell of beer, of wood smoke, of roasting meat and fish, of wool and leather impregnated with grease and sweat, all the fine compounded flavor of conviviality and food assailed the nostrils of the stranger with such a promise of good things behind the closed door that the walls of his stomach drew together painfully. She waited for him to speak, hugging her arms against the cold. The stranger took off his wide-brimmed felt hat and held it under his right arm as he inquired humbly if she were the new mistress of the Golden Lion. Her eyes went briefly to the sign above their heads and then down to his coat, his shabby feet, as she answered yes, that she was the mistress.

"Then could you give me," said he, "food and lodging for the night?"

Her eyes continued to appraise him, and although her presence was surrounded with warmth and the scent of hospitality, the eyes were reserved and unfriendly. The corner of her mouth lifted slightly as she answered:

"As a guest, or as a beggar?"

"Well, tonight," he said, looking down also at his broken boots, and then, with embarrassment, at her cold, bright eyes, "tonight I am out of funds. But it might not always be that way," he hastened to add. "And I am as near starved as ever I was."

"But tonight," said she, "I have guests—a wedding party—and the house is very crowded. I have no room for beggars."

Chapter One

I have been a soldier," he said.

"We have no love for soldiers in these parts," she answered.

"You should feed the hungry and lay yourself up treasure in heaven," he said then, but not as if he believed very greatly in such treasure. "There will be plenty of scrapings if there is a party," he added with more conviction.

She continued to appraise him with her eyes, as if she might find something to make her alter her refusal. That he was very tired was evident in the gray look of the skin and the drawn features. He had not been shaved in a long time. The lower part of his face was black with stubble, and the lank black hair, streaked slightly with gray, fell down in straggling ends upon the collar of his doublet. He wore no linen, but his doublet had once been exceeding fine, of a heavy padded crimson satin quilted in a diamond pattern with gold thread, and having skirts in the French style. It was filthy now, and splitting at the elbow. He might well have been a soldier. He wore above this fine French garment a heavy leather jerkin, and across this, diagonally over one shoulder and down to his belt, such a leather band as might have carried a pistol and knife. The left sleeve of the doublet was folded and tucked within the leather jerkin. It was empty from just above the elbow. His ragged serge breeches consorted ill with the crimson doublet. The hat which he held under his right arm was green with age and lacked both feather and buckle. The little green eyes in the fatigued countenance were fastened to those of the mistress of the inn with a look from which all expression had been drained save that of hunger. Neither the servility nor the fear remained. The appeal was too intense; she wished him away from the inn.

"We have no love for soldiers or for beggars," she repeated. "You had best be going along."

She had turned away and would have pressed down the latch save for his bitter exclamation.

"Going along! As if I hadn't been going along for weeks now, and maybe months. So when I come back to my own parish, where I may be rich again someday —yes, rich and honorable—they tell me to be going along." Then, as if the changes in the landscape might have indeed deceived him, he inquired, "This is truly Aalsö parish, isn't it?"

"Truly enough," she said, "and Aalsö village a few miles down the road if you keep going."

"Then could you tell me one thing," he said, "before you shut the door on me—just one thing?"

"And that's what?" she asked.

"You know of one Morten Bruus?"

"Indeed, why not?" she answered shortly.

"Well, then, is he living or dead?"

"Dead," she answered. "Dead since before St. John's Day."

The beggar, still holding his battered hat in his right hand, lifted his hand and rubbed the back of it slowly across his mouth, backward and forward several times, whether, as it seemed, to partly hide the smile on his lips or simply to express his satisfaction at the news. The satisfaction was most plain, and horrible. It shone in the small green eyes, grown strangely bright in that dulled countenance. At last he said:

"Dead almost half a year, you promise me?"

"Surely dead, dead as a stone," she answered.

"Bear with me," said the beggar. "It is a comfort to me to hear it said."

"And to many another," she replied. "Well, give you good night."

This time she pressed her finger on the latch, and, in the silence, he heard it sprung.

"Wait one minute," he cried. "If you will not take me in tonight, where will I bide? You would not, mistress, be so unkind as to shut a poor soldier out in the wet and the cold. You see for yourself how cold it is going to be. Is there no charity left in Jutland?"

The mistress of the Golden Lion shrugged her shoulders. "You might ask of the pastor," she said.

"The pastor?" said the beggar. Then, as if the name were dredged from a deep, muddy memory, "That would be Pastor Peder Korf."

"No," she said briskly. "Peder Korf is dead, God rest him. The pastor now is Juste Pedersen, and a very good man he is, too."

"Pastor Juste," repeated the beggar. "Is he a kind man, and hospitable?"

"Kind as Sören Qvist," she answered, pushing the door open a crack.

"So!" cried the beggar suddenly. "And did you know Pastor Sören?"

"How would I have known him?" said the woman. "I was not weaned in his day. It is only a way of speaking they have in these parts. Kind as Sören Qvist, generous as Sören Qvist—so the phrase goes. That is just the way they talk."

"And do they never say angry as Sören Qvist?" said the beggar with a faint, evil grin.

The woman looked at him in some surprise, but made no answer, as if the question deserved none. The beggar, for a moment, seemed disposed to inquire further into this way of speaking. Then he settled his old hat on his head and, peering at her slyly from under the brim, said, in a beggar's manner:

"I am a stranger in these parts—at least, I've been gone so long I'm as good as a stranger. But does the parsonage still stand where it used to?"

"Why would it be changed?" she said.

He did not reply, but looked at her oddly again from under the brim of his hat before he resumed his journey. In spite of the cold, the inn wife remained to watch him, her hand still on the latch, until his limping figure had rounded the bend in the road and quite disappeared from view. As she stood so, the door was pulled open behind her, and a man, coming to stand beside her, dropped his arm about her shoulders.

"What keeps you so long, lass?" he said. He was a well-favored fellow in his middle forties, his face ruddy and toughened, marked by few lines, and his thick blond hair fell evenly on a clean white linen collar. The inn wife turned toward him and smiled, and continued to look at him as if she were rinsing her vision of an unpleasant image.

"Only a beggar," she said at last, "but a filthy ani-

mal, a son of the Bad One. He was asking about Morten Bruus. And now it seems to me that he looked
oddly like Morten. Had Morten yet a brother?"

He shook his head. "Only the one you've heard of.
And that was two too many whelps of the same breed-
ing," he said.

"He seemed pleased to hear of his death."

"Even the beggars of the roads," said the man.

In the room behind them someone began to sing, a
good rich voice in a rolling stave that was taken up by
the other merrymakers. The inn wife and her com-
panion still stood without, the light from the open door
pouring out around them and blurring upon the heavy
air. The man presently said, without raising his voice,
but his voice, close to the woman's ear, distinct in
every word:

"Morten Bruus, may God send him, though dead, a
lasting and a feeling body to suffer all the torments of
the flesh forever and ever. May his skin be torn from
him in little pieces, each one no bigger than a finger-
nail. May worms devour his bowels, and his stomach
be filled with broken glass, and the roof of his mouth
scorched, his eyelids cut off, and his eyes open upon
the fire that surrounds him, world without end. May
God never permit him to repent of his life in order that
he may never be forgiven for any deed of it. Amen."

This unangered expression of a quiet, impersonal,
and well-considered hatred came forth phrase by
phrase in leisurely fashion to the accompaniment of
the merry trolling within doors. "Amen," said the inn
wife, and the music continued.

The one-armed beggar went on toward the village of Aalsö. After the nearness of warmth and nourishment withheld, the evening seemed increasingly lonely and the cold more penetrating. The twilight faded so slowly that the lessening of the light seemed rather a thickening of the air, as those night vapors considered full of harm and contagion gathered in the hollows of the road, in the low bushes, and in the shadows of the beechwoods. The fawn and umber tones of the dried weeds, the sandy road, in the gentle landscape were gradually obscured, and the faint pale gold of the stubble fields had no counterpart of pale gold in the sky. The beggar, in his soiled crimson doublet like a dying coal, moved on laboriously between the fields and hedges and came at last to Aalsö village. It was like the other villages of Jutland, diminished, closed, and dark, although so early in the night. It was inhabited, however, he could tell. Smoke issued from its chimnes. He turned from the highroad to a lane through a plowed and planted field and, feeling the landscape ever more familiar in its small details, crossed a plank bridge above a brook and found himself before a small whitewashed half-timbered dwelling.

It was surely the Aalsö parsonage; it was smaller than he remembered it. He had not come here as often as he had been sent, when he was a boy, but he remembered it. He stepped close to the door and knocked, and, as he waited for a sound from within, he put up his right hand and touched the blackened straw of the thatch which came down shawl-like about the doorway.

There should have been a jog in the wall to the right of him, and the higher roof of the unit which he remembered as the New Room. This was gone, and had been gone for some time; the older part of the house had been rethatched, and that portion of the wall of the New Room which remained had been leveled off at shoulder height and made to be the wall of a courtyard. He looked over the wall and saw that grass had grown between the bricks of the old floor. On the farther side of the courtyard was a small byre with a half-open doorway. As he looked, an old woman came through the doorway, carrying a ruffled brown hen under each arm. She did not see him at once, for she was picking her steps upon the uneven bricks; when she did glance up and observe him, she was frightened. She stopped short, then stepped back against the wall of the byre, holding her two brown hens in a closer embrace. For her, the outline of the broad and rakish hat, the long black hair, the gleam of crimson of the

21

French doublet, meant the presence of a soldier, and, like the inn wife, she had no love for soldiers. However, after her first fright, she came forward staunchly, passed through the swinging wooden gate in the side wall, and so around to the spot where the stranger waited.

The stranger had never been skilled at begging, but whereas he had presented himself to the inn wife as one who had been a soldier, he now had wit enough to present himself as a beggar. He took off his battered hat and asked for food and shelter. There was a certain honesty in his servility; he was half starved, and shaken with fatigue.

The old woman had a kind face, a face full of wrinkles in a soft, fresh-colored skin. Her blue eyes were round and gentle, her head bound in a cap of dull blue camlet. The line of white which framed her face was not linen, but the smooth margin of white hair. She said:

"Do you come from far?"

"As far as from Hamburg within the last month. Before that, from Bohemia. But I was a boy in Aalsö parish. I did my catechism here," he expatiated, "with Pastor Peder Korf."

"Did you so?" she said, taking a step forward. "But did you look to find Pastor Peder?"

"They tell me that he is dead."

She nodded.

"And that Pastor Juste is kind as Sören Qvist."

She did not smile at this, but nodded again, seriously.

"Yes," she said, "he is kind. If you will wait now, I will go tell him that you are here."

She edged by him and pushed the door open with her elbow, being careful not to joggle her hens, and pushed it shut again from within. She returned after a little time and let him into the kitchen of Aalsö parsonage.

The room was so dark that at first he saw nothing but the light of the fire on the raised hearth, but it was warm, warm and snug. He felt with pleasure the closeness of the walls, the nearness of the heavy beams in the low ceiling. He had been too long out of doors under a sky crowded either with wind or with massing fog. It was fine to feel a roof close over his head. He made his way across the brick floor to a stool near the hearth and sat down, holding out his hands to the fire. The old woman busied herself in the darker corner of the kitchen. He heard her wooden shoes clapping on the bricks, the swish and swing of her heavy skirts, and, behind him, the rustling of feathers, a few sleepy clucks. In a short time the old woman came bearing a wooden plate on which was a loaf of bread, uncut. She dragged a small bench near the hearth, set the plate upon it, and stood back, winding her hands in her dark blue apron. The beggar looked from the loaf to the old woman, standing there solidly with the light from the fire on her face, on her white smock and yellow bodice and her blue apron, watching him. The light was golden upon the glazed side of the loaf. He eyed it, then, since she did not move, reached out his hand toward it.

"Stop!" cried the old woman, dropping her apron

and reaching toward the loaf herself. "You would not take my good loaf in your dirty hand, like that! Where is your knife? Cannot you cut yourself a piece, like a Christian man?"

"I have no knife," said the beggar, taken aback. "If I had had a knife I would have traded it for a can of beer at the inn. So help me, I have no knife, and I could not use it with great skill if I had it."

The old woman considered him. "Turn toward the fire," she commanded him. Obediently he slewed around on his seat. "Very well," she said, "you carry no knife on your back at least, and"—she hesitated a little, as if in slight apology—"I did not at first notice that your sleeve was empty. I saw a Spanish soldier," she continued, "came with Wallenstein's men, had a belt like yours over his shoulder and carried a long dagger in it, on his back. I will cut the bread. Were you ever a soldier?"

"Until I lost my arm," he said. "But what can a man do with only one arm? Since then I am a beggar."

When she had cut the bread, she gave him a slice of cheese as well, and she noted how the hand that reached for it shook with eagerness, and how, as the man ate, he seemed to forget where he was, and everything except the taste of food in his mouth. Watching him, as she had watched so many others here in the pastor's kitchen, she felt her fear give way to pity, and having filled a pewter mug with beer, she set it close to the coals to warm. Starving men, starving animals, for over forty years this had been one of her duties, to feed them and to give them shelter. The bounty was less great now than in the old days because there was less to give. Still, what the pastor could bestow was for the homeless, and she had the bestowing of it.

"You can sleep in the byre," she said. "It is clean enough, and the beasts make it warm."

He consumed the bread and cheese to the last crumb, drank the warm beer, and sat, with his hand about the mug, staring into the fire for a few minutes before he spoke again.

Then he said, half to himself, "I have nothing, you see, not even a knife. Nothing at all but the rags I wear. But it may not always be so." The warm beer in an empty stomach made him feel sorry for himself. It was pleasant to be sorry for himself beside a warm fire. Slowly his mind began to work again, and he remembered why he had come back to Aalsö. Surely it was not to study Luther's Catechism in the New Room, which was now gone. But he had needed to see Pastor Peder. He said to the old woman cautiously, yet as if it did not concern him greatly, "Do you know one Morten Bruus?"

"Aye," she answered without enthusiasm. "He was at one time of this parish."

"Then he is dead? As I hear?"

"Yes, dead, and no one the sadder."

"Surely not myself," said the beggar. "Well, we cannot all be mourned."

"We need not be hated," said she.

"So he was hated, eh?" said the beggar.

"If you know his name, you know that he was hated," she replied.

25

She rose to put away the remnant of the loaf in a wooden chest on the farther side of the fire, and he watched her regretfully but did not venture to protest. Beyond the chest was a door, the door to the parson's bedroom, as he remembered, and in the wall beyond it, at right angles, was the alcove where the housekeeper's pillows and quilts were piled. In all the years that he had been away he had not paused once to try to remember this room, but now that he was here again everything returned to his memory as being just as it had been, except that the door to the New Room was now walled up. As for the old woman, he seemed somehow to remember her, and yet the more he thought, the more it came to him that the pastor's housekeeper had been a smaller woman, with sharp black eyes and a quick hand. She had not had the patience of Peder Korf.

"So the old pastor is dead," he said at length. "Was it long since?"

The old woman seated herself on the bench in which she had bestowed the bread.

"Long since indeed," she said. "I was young then. Well, at least I was but in my forties, and today that's young." She sighed, and the beggar inquired:

"It was not old age then that did away with the pastor. Like enough it was the plague."

"A plague of Catholic bandits," said the old woman. "A gang of Wallenstein's men. May God never forgive them."

The beggar considered. "Yes, that was long since I had not been long out of Jutland then."

26

Chapter Two

"Torstenson's men were thieves and vandals also," said the old woman, "but at least they were not Catholics but merely Swedes. Ah, but Jutland has suffered, suffered for all of Denmark. I wonder why God was willing to have us suffer so. But Wallenstein's men were the worst."

The beggar said nothing, and the old woman, speaking out of an old and deep sadness, continued:

"Everyone fled to the islands that had strength to move, or nearly everyone. Pastor wouldn't go, and I stayed with Pastor. But when they came, and we saw the flames about Aalsö village and the nearby farms, I ran into the woods. Pastor stayed by the place. He was a brave man, Pastor Peder Korf. He said that his people might be running to him for help, and he meant to stay and protect them." She paused, and the beggar kept silent, his head tipped forward, watching her from under his black brows with his little greenish eyes. She drew a deep breath and said, "When I came back to the place, Pastor was hanging from the beech tree, close by the door there, hanging by his beard—you remember his thick brown beard—and cut in many places; and he was dead. The house was burning. The cattle gone. Each last little hen was gone. There was a fire set in the barley field, that was ripe for mowing. I came back and stood here in front of this house and looked at him, and saw the turf all bloody under where he was hanging. They did that because they thought to mock him, to mock a priest for wearing a beard. You remember how thick and strong a beard he had, and how he used to tug at it with his fingers when he was thinking? The fire burned almost all night. Then, before morning, it began to rain. And so, year before last, when Torstenson came, we all hid. Pastor Juste went through the village and gathered all his people together, and we hid in the beechwood, and so we are still alive. The Swedes burned much and stole everything. Still, it was not quite so bad as when the Catholics came." She stopped speaking. Then she said, "That God should make such men."

"I was with Wallenstein's men," the beggar muttered, as if to himself. "I was with them in Bohemia. But," he added piously, "when they took the road to Jutland, I left them. Not for anything would I have come back to soldier in Jutland."

"God may take that into consideration when your time comes," said the housekeeper, "that you burned houses only in another country. Well, it is late. Come. I will show you where you can sleep."

The beggar picked up his hat from the floor beside him and stood up, unwillingly. He looked at the embers on the hearth, red-golden, translucent, showing, some of them, the exact shape of the twig or branch, transmuted but intact, and all veiled in a blue flickering.

"A pity to leave so good a fire," he said.

The housekeeper stood with her hand on the door, waiting for him.

"I never thought to give food or drink to one of Wallenstein's men," was all she said.

"Well, thanks for the food," said the soldier, "all the same."

He moved limping toward the door, his hat in his

hand, but turned once more to look back at the glowing hearth.

"I can surely see Pastor in the morning?" he asked.

The old woman answered by a nod.

"This Morten Bruus," he said again, delaying his departure. "If all the farms in Jutland have been twice robbed, I suppose he can no longer be very rich. Were his buildings fired, like the others?"

"Oh no," the old woman answered, "he had the devil's protection on him, if you ask me. His buildings were never fired, nor his fields trampled, and he died the richest man in Vejlby parish, or in this one, too."

"Do you say so? Well then." The beggar considered this information and then inquired with an air of great caution, "Did he leave a rich widow, this fellow Bruus?"

"Never a wife, never a widow, nor any kith or kin," said the old woman.

"Nor any friend? Did he leave his goods in gift to a friend?"

"Living or dead, he never gave anything to anyone, that I ever heard of," she answered him. "You are very curious about Morten Bruus. Did you know him ever?"

The beggar stretched out his one arm in a gesture of exultation.

"That is what I shall tell the pastor in the morning," he said. "I shall be rich. I have been the poorest and now I'll be the richest. I am Morten's brother Niels." He gave a short laugh, the sound of which rung against the copper pans hanging upon the farther wall and echoed sharply back, with neither mirth nor friendship.

The old woman lifted her head and drew back a step, exactly as if she had been struck in the face.

"So then," she said with scorn. "Perhaps you were never with Wallenstein's men, either. Perhaps I may forgive you that. A pig bit off your arm, doubtless, and you have come all the way from Aalborg, perhaps, but you have never been out of Jutland in all your life. This is a fine story about the brother of Morten Bruus, but you have come to the wrong house with it." She pushed the door wide open and stood waiting for him to leave. The cold air poured in upon them from the blackness without. "You should be sent away for such lying," she said, "but the pastor has said you might sleep with the beasts. Well, good night," she added impatiently.

But the beggar stood his ground.

"I am not lying," he said. "I am really the brother of Morten Bruus. I can prove it, since it's true."

"You are Niels Bruus?" said the old woman.

"Niels, the brother of Morten."

"Oh, what a scurvy liar," said the old woman with deeper scorn. "What a poor and pitiful liar. Listen to me. With my own eyes I saw the body of Niels Bruus dug out of the ground many, many years ago, and he was so long dead he stank. Yet you come and tell me that you are Niels Bruus."

The effect of these words upon the beggar was strange. He stared at the old woman with eyes gone blank with astonishment, and his jaw sagged. Then he began to grin, a stupid evil grin, and then he broke into laughter. He struck his hat against his thigh to

30

emphasize his enjoyment of her statement, and his laughter, filling the small room, seemed to her the most stupid, the most evil sound she had ever heard.

"Stop," she cried. "Be quiet," and stamped upon the brick floor with her wooden shoes, opposing one noise to another, in a kind of panic. "Are you gone crazy?"

The beggar paused in his laughter to ask, "And was my face all battered, mistress?" Then, as he saw her blench from him, "And did you see a fine lead earring in this ear?" and he pointed, with his hat, to his left ear.

The old woman's face filled with horror. She lifted a hand and crossed herself, slowly.

"Tell me," said the beggar, "did Parson Sören see me too? And smell me, ha? Tell me, who dug me up and where was I buried?"

The old woman, having retreated from him a few steps, stopped and, composing herself, her face full of loathing, placed both hands firmly on her hips and replied in a steady voice, as if she were exorcising a demon:

"I saw in Pastor Sören's garden Morten Bruus himself strike the spade into the ground and uncover the body of Niels, his brother; I, and many others. It would take more than a beggar from Aalborg to make me think other than that Niels is dead and buried in Vejlby churchyard. Do you think to be rich with Morten's money? Oh, what a fool!"

"But I know that the face was battered, and that the body wore my clothes, and that my lead earring was in the left ear, yes, just as I used to wear it. How do you think I know all that?"

31

The woman gave a shrug of the shoulders.

"Anyone can know all that," she answered.

"Well, but I know more," said the beggar. His voice became quiet and sly. "I know that Morten buried the body. That is why he could find it. It was," he said, ever more sly and confidential, "a little joke that Morten played on Pastor Sören. Morten did not love the pastor, if you remember."

His eyes were fixed upon the round blue eyes of the old woman, and he thought he saw a horrified belief grow slowly in those honest blue eyes.

"Yes," he cried triumphantly, "a little joke that Morten played upon the pastor, and I can tell you all about it."

The old woman turned her back upon him abruptly and crossed the kitchen to the pastor's door. She knocked, her back still turned upon the beggar, then entered the pastor's room and closed the door behind her.

The beggar could not stand still for excitement. He limped to the hearth and stood staring briefly at the golden embers under their veil of blue. Then he limped across the room to the wall in which once had been the door to the New Room. With that door gone, the kitchen seemed very small; aye, and with the door to the parson's study closed. He looked at all the cupboards with shut doors and tried to remember in which one the old woman had locked the cheese; then, growing aware that his feet hurt him, he returned to the stool by the hearth and drew off his boots. The bricks were cold to his feet, but the air of the room was warmer than the wet and broken leather. He began to rub his feet with his hand, and was sitting so, stooped by the fire, when the door to the study swung open, and the old woman came back into the kitchen.

She was followed by an old man in a loose black gown that was furred at the neck but shabby. A fringe of white hair showed about the rim of his black skullcap. His face was lean and his figure slight and somewhat stooped. He moved forward silently, after the clacking footsteps of the housekeeper, because he was in his stockinged feet, and the quietness of his advance, together with his appearace of great age and gentleness, produced a certain awe within the beggar. The hilarity that had possessed him died away, although the excitement remained. He stood up and bobbed his head respectfully to the old man.

"Pastor Juste Pedersen," said the old woman, "here is the man who claims to be the brother of Morten Bruus."

"Sit down, my friend," said the old man. "Sit down, Vibeke."

He motioned toward the bench by the fire, and the housekeeper seated herself as she had been formerly. The pastor drew up a stool and seated himself so that he could face both the housekeeper and the beggar. The light from the hearth shone full upon him, gilding the shabby robe, the bosses of the high, bony forehead, the lean hands with heavy knuckles which lay quietly upon his knees.

"Now then," said Pastor Juste sensibly, "let us get at the truth of this matter." He looked the beggar over,

33

unhurriedly, with the eye of a man who has had much experience at reading countenances, and the intense excitement held in check by the advance of authority did not escape him. "Vibeke Andersdaughter," he said, "tells me that you claim to have been formerly of my parish, and that you now are come to demand the fortune of Morten Bruus. Tell me, how did it happen that you left this country in the first place?"

"Morten sent me away," said the beggar.

"Ah! And when was it you left?"

The beggar considered.

"It was after harvest, and before snow. And the year, it was before Lutter-am-Barenberge. It was the autumn before the summer when the King was defeated at Lutter. Yes, that was it."

"Were you perhaps at Lutter?" asked the pastor.

"I was at Lutter, yes."

"Was it there that you lost your arm?"

"No, that was much later. I was at Lutter, with Wallenstein."

"You mean to say that you fought against your King?" said the pastor.

"Well, Morten told me to get clear out of Jutland. So I went into Germany. And what could I do? It was winter; no one wanted a farm hand. But there was always fighting. Besides, Wallenstein paid much better than the King."

"It has nothing to do with the case," said the pastor, "still, I should be interested to know where you did lose your arm."

"That was at Lützen," said the beggar. "That was in

'thirty-two, I mind. We had a bad time at Lützen. And since then I beg."

"It was a sorrowful thing for Jutland," said the pastor, "the defeat of the King. Now, that was 1626, in August. So that I reckon that you left Jutland in the fall of 1625. You have been gone then full one and twenty years, and more than half that time you have been a beggar. Knowing that Morten was rich, and could have given you a home, why did you not return to Jutland, after Lützen?"

"I was afraid of Morten," said the beggar without hesitation.

The pastor considered this.

"Did you then wrong your brother?"

"Oh no, Pastor, I never wronged him. I only did whatever he told me, and I was afraid of him. And he told me to stay out of Jutland."

"Then," inquired the pastor, "how did you come to hear of his death? Is the name of Morten Bruus known as far away as Lützen?"

"Well," said the beggar, "as you say, twenty-one years is a long time, and I speak like a Jutlander still. People are much kinder to a man who doesn't talk like a stranger. So in the end I came back to Slesvig, just a bit over the border, to hear a bit of natural talk. I was in Slesvig on a farm in the Black parish, and there was a man there who had once traded a horse from Morten. He had heard that Morten was dead, and he was telling his wife. So I heard it. So I came north. In Aebeltoft I heard it too. So it seemed safe to come home."

"It is true that you speak like a Jutlander," said the pastor. "Still, that alone is hardly enough to prove you Morten's brother. Did anyone tell you that you resembled Morten?"

The beggar grinned and showed his blackened teeth.

"I was never so handsome as Morten," he said.

"You were baptized in this parish?"

"But surely."

"How old were you when you left Jutland?"

"I was eighteen years, I think."

"And how old was Morten at that time?"

The beggar counted on his fingers.

"Morten was twenty-six years then. We were living at Ingvorstrup then, in Vejlby parish."

"Since Peder Korf is gone, could you name anyone in this parish, or in Vejlby, who knew you when you were a boy?"

The beggar had to think a little while, and the first name that he brought forth caused the pastor to glance at Vibeke.

"It is a pity," said the pastor, "that Erland Neilsen of Ingvorstrup was dead before my day. Think again."

The beggar then, without great hesitation, tried half a dozen names, but at each of them the pastor shook his head.

"All these are either dead, or gone away, years since. Consider now, it is not enough that you know these names, and the ages of Niels and Morten. You could have learned any of this over a can of beer at the last inn. If you are to prove yourself Morten's brother you must think of someone who can stand before us and swear to recognizing you."

"Well, then," said the beggar slowly, very slowly, "there could be Sören Qvist, who was pastor at Vejlby."

At this the pastor and Vibeke again exchanged glances. Then the pastor rose.

"That about settles it," he said.

"Settles what?" said the beggar.

"That you are not Niels Bruus. Look here, my friend. I am sorry for you. Since you are crippled and homeless, it is a great temptation to seek for wealth that does not belong to you. Still, you should know better than to set yourself up as being a man long since dead. There are those who would bring punishment upon you for pretending to be other than you are. Take my advice, and say no more about it."

The beggar also rose to his feet.

"That is all very well to say talk no more about it, but I am telling the truth. I think I know who I am. And I have as much right to Morten's money as any man alive. Perhaps you will be telling me Pastor Sören is gone too. Well, I forgot that he would be an old man, a very old man, even, but he was strong and hale when last I saw him, and he would remember me. Anna Sörensdaughter would remember me too, and she will not be old."

He spoke vehemently, so much so that the pastor was constrained to lift his hand to quiet him. But Vibeke, the old Vibeke, now came forward and said:

"Pastor, I have been thinking. He has, as you have noticed, a strong look of Morten Bruus. There was always something we never understood about the

37

whole affair. God help us all, I was sure there was witchcraft in it. God protect us, but indeed I think he is Niels. Make him stay and tell us what Morten buried, was it a dead cat or a wax baby like the wax babies of Kalmar. Tryg Thorwaldsen would know him, and Tryg is still alive."

The pastor turned to the beggar.

"Do you know a man by the name of Tryg Thorwaldsen?" he asked.

"The magistrate from Rosmos?" said the beggar. "Yes, I know him. Yes, he would know me. He was not one of my friends, but he is an honest man."

"Are you willing to be questioned by him?" said the pastor.

"Yes, yes," said the beggar. "Yes, I am willing. He is an honest man, and he will see that I come by my money. After all, I have a right to my money."

"Then, in the morning," said the pastor, "I will ride over and fetch him."

"Oh, fetch him tonight!" cried the old woman.

"What need?" said Pastor Juste. "The man can sleep here, no matter who he is, and in the morning I can fetch Thorwaldsen. Or we can go together, all of us, to Rosmos."

"Tonight, tonight!" cried the old Vibeke, catching at his arm with both her hands. The hands dug into his arm as if to steady themselves, but the pastor could feel how they trembled, and turning to look into her face, he saw that the blue eyes were almost black, the pupils distended in a great fear. He smiled to reassure her, laying his hand over hers.

"He will not vanish like an apparition," he said.

"Ah, but he might," she whispered. "You do not understand, you were not here when it happened."

"But he has much to gain by staying," said the pastor.

"Do you think I will run away, mistress?" said the beggar. "Oh no, oh no. Who would run away from a fortune like that of my brother Morten?"

"God might strike you dead before morning," retorted the old woman. "Or the devil might put out a hand for you. Then we should never know." But to the pastor she said, pleading, her heart in her voice, "Those of us who loved him have a right to know how it happened. Tryg has a right to know."

The beggar interrupted harshly, "I have already told you how it happened. God's wounds, the trouble is you don't believe me."

"That is true," said the old woman. "With one breath I believe you are Niels. With the next, you are only a beggar of the roads has picked up part of an old story. How can I sleep in peace until someone else tells me, 'Yes, it is Niels,' or 'No, it is not Niels; Niels is in Vejlby churchyard'?"

"It is indeed an old story," said Pastor Juste.

"For you it is," said Vibeke. "For me it is as if it had happened yesterday, and my heart aches, as it did then, and I am afraid, as I was then. I beg of you, go for Tryg tonight. Or, faith, I will go myself."

The parson gave a half groan.

"It shall never be said of me I sent you on an errand at this hour of the night. I will go myself," he said.

Judge Tryg Thorwaldsen was entertaining guests, but he left his place at the table to greet the pastor from Aalsö. From the door at the head of the stairs, for the dining room was on the first floor, the pastor surveyed the company seated about the long oak table. The room was narrow, paneled with oak. On the one side a row of narrow casement windows overlooked the street. This night their leaded panes shone like black water, or, where the glass was set unevenly, caught the candlelight like small mirrors. The center of the table was a blaze of candles, the faces of the company bright in the glow, all the backs in silhouette. The light shone upon the silver tankards and crystal glasses, the ruddy cheeks, the well-combed hair, the fine white linen collars, upon a few starched and fluted ruffs, on good broadcloth and velvet, and, where there was velvet, upon some broad gold chains.

Thorwaldsen himself was in velvet, with a single gold chain; he wore a collar of white linen with the new square lappets. A man in his late forties, his hair was more gray than flaxen, and he wore it cut very short for the times. He had an extraordinarily long and bony face, with a wide, pleasant mouth and a long, bony chin; his eyes were honest and intelligent, and of a blue so steady and bright that they redeemed the general homeliness of his other features.

"I have guests of some importance," he said courteously, "but if the matter is urgent, I can come with you."

"It is not that I place great credence in the story of this beggar," explained the pastor, "but that my housekeeper is distressed beyond reason."

"I have an old regard for Vibeke Andersdaughter," said Thorwaldsen. "I will come at once. Unless we can persuade you to stop for a glass of burgundy."

"I thank you," said the pastor, "but I am truly uneasy at leaving her. I should like to return at once."

He waited for Thorwaldsen in the close darkness at the foot of the stairs, and when the magistrate had joined him they stepped together out of doors, still waiting for their horses to be brought. The outer darkness was less intense than that within doors. A pallor overhung the housetops, and from this pallor a few stars emerged, like snow that did not fall. The night was very cold. The pastor protested at the delay.

"You need not be so uneasy about Vibeke," said Thorwaldsen. "She is still hale, and I warrant her a match for any one-armed man."

"It is not that," the pastor answered. "She is afraid of something unnatural. I too have the feeling that something evil is encamped by my hearth. It is hard to explain.

"I am not sure this beggar is malevolent. Rather, he seems to me stupid, only. I am reminded of what I was once taught concerning the nature of demons, that they are demons by virtue of their very incompleteness. The evil of this man lies in what he lacks.

"Do you think he could actually be Niels Bruus?"

"I have been convinced for twenty-one years," said Thorwaldsen, "that I saw Niels buried in Vejlby churchyard."

"He has a very strong look of Morten Bruus," said the old pastor.

"That might well be," said the other. "Bruus was not an outlander. Although he had no close living kindred, he had any number of forty-second cousins."

The horses were brought then, and they mounted. For a time they rode together. Thorwaldsen said:

"Twenty-one years is a long time, and yet tonight it looks not half so long to me as it seemed when I was twenty-one and looked forward into it."

"It is a great pity," said the pastor, jogging by his side, "to have to dig up and bring to light, as it were, this tragedy so long buried and, in some part, forgotten. It must be painful to you, and I am sorry that I have to recall it to you."

Thorwaldsen said, simply, "It is the one real sorrow of my life."

The pastor sighed and said, "You must have loved your wife very much."

"She was not my wife," answered Thorwaldsen. "We were betrothed."

Chapter Three

"It is all the same thing," said the pastor, in the innocence of his heart.

"It is not the same at all," answered the other, "because if she had been my wife, she would not have left me. At least, I think that she would not have done so."

"You must pardon me," said the pastor, "if I am not well informed. I was not in Jutland at the time. As you may remember, I came only in 'twenty-nine."

"I am not very good at remembering dates," said Tryg Thorwaldsen, "but I do remember that you came after the peace. Well, you must have heard plenty of it, even then."

"Very much," said the pastor, "and sometimes things contradictory. It was even then taking on the shape of a legend. As was most natural. But it was so much spoken of that when I heard this beggar call for Sören Qvist as a witness, I concluded that he must know nothing whatever about the true story. In short, I took him to be a fraud."

"Could he not," said the magistrate, "have pretended to know nothing of the fate of Sören Qvist in order to assume an innocence? He would hardly care to put his neck into a noose even for Morten's fortune."

"You think it hazardous, then, to be Niels Bruus?" asked the pastor.

"There is that possibility," said Tryg.

"I think he has no sense of such a hazard," said the pastor. "Nor are his wits nimble enough for such a calculation. But consider, that if Morten sent his brother out of Jutland before the corpse was dug from the ground, then his brother would not be likely to know anything of what befell thereafter. It seems to me this beggar may be Niels."

"I was acquainted with Niels, living," said Thorwaldsen. "I never doubted but that I saw him buried in Vejlby churchyard."

The pastor did not reply. The finality in the magistrate's words was matched with doubt in his own mind, but, after all, he had taken Thorwaldsen from his warm room and his companions not so much for the sake of a beggar who might or might not come into a fortune as to quiet the fear of old Vibeke.

When the road grew narrow, the magistrate took the lead. Overhead more stars appeared, blurred and bright, although on earth the mist remained thick; it lay clouded among the trees and over the fields; the breath from the nostrils of the horses showed mist within mist. The air stung and clung to the face. Perhaps it was clearing overhead in preparation for a more intense cold. The pastor, still thinking of Vibeke, wished they might travel faster.

As for Tryg Thorwaldsen, he pushed forward through the darkness and mist as if he were pushing through time, but backward, year by year, slowly back to his young manhood and the vehemence and vigor of his youth. Through the darkness faces appeared to him, touched with spring sunlight, touched with tears, and an old sorrow and longing that he thought he had put aside resumed its old power. He thought, "The past is never dead. Within ourselves it becomes a part of ourselves, and lives as we do, and beyond us it becomes a part of the popular speech.

44

Chapter Three

When the story is forgotten, the phrase survives. 'As kind as Sören Qvist.' I heard the saying only this morning in Vejlby market." It was usual. He had heard it so often that he had not paused to remark it, or to consider it as a herald of any return of the past. Then, might the past return? he asked himself.

He drew rein suddenly and, turning in his saddle, waited for the pastor to overtake him.

"I was abrupt, Pastor Juste," he said. "Pardon me. It is incredible to me that your beggar should be Niels, yet, if it is so, I shall have a search to make through every village and farm, yes, and every city in Skaane, though it should take me the rest of my life."

"And for whom would you search?" inquired the old pastor hesitantly, hearing the passion in the quiet voice.

"Why, for Anna Sörensdaughter." Thorwaldsen spoke very low. The name drifted to the old man, through the darkness, through the chill air, like some petal loosened from a flowering bough remote in spring.

"Through every village, every farm," said Thorwaldsen again.

After Vibeke had seen the pastor cloaked and mounted and upon his way to Vejlby, she brought fresh wood to the fire and then, latching the door against a slight wind that seemed to be rising from the west, returned to her seat behind the fire. The beggar had not stirred from his place on the other side of the hearth.

Vibeke was learning afresh that doubt is a dreadful torment. And twenty-one years is a long time over which to recall a face of which you never took especial note. The excitement which had possessed the beggar a short time before had died away, and a greater fatigue had taken its place. He stared into the fire with eyes grown dull. Vibeke, watching him, thought again that the narrow forehead and the long nose with the remarkably long and narrow nostrils were very like the features of Niels Bruus. But the lines of the face were all cut much deeper than in the face she remembered, and the black stubble of the unshaved beard darkened them about the mouth and chin in an unre-

46

membered way. The lank black hair was like that of
Niels. But, on the other hand, now that so much de-
pended upon it, the likeness seemed not so great. And
he had been one of Wallenstein's men, Wallenstein
who had been for two years and a half the scourge and
terror of Jutland. He had said that he had no knife,
but you could never trust a man who had been with
Wallenstein. Perhaps this story of his was just a trick
to get money, as the parson had suggested, or even,
since he was so near starved and had been turned from
the inn, a device to get a meal and a lodging for the
night. She watched him carefully, lest he slip his hand
into his pocket, or into his breast, and come forth with
a knife, and the more she watched him, the more certain she became that he was only an impostor, and
she wished that she were not alone in the house with
him. She wished that she could send him out to the
byre and lock the door upon him. But he would not
stir; she knew that. He was waiting for the return of
Parson Juste and the magistrate, and he was there by
her own demand. He was calm enough about it now
for anyone who knew himself to be a fraud. You would
think he might be frightened at the thought of being
questioned by so great a man as Judge Thorwaldsen.
Indeed, he had not seemed pleased at the idea. Perhaps he would yet be frightened, and slip out before
they came. Or perhaps he meant to strike her down
and rob the house and escape. She watched him very
carefully, and she reckoned that, even if he drew a
knife, she could seize the parson's stool and strike
him with it.

And then, the more she watched him, the more the face again began to resemble that of Niels, and the beggar became a man who had been dug from the ground before her very eyes. She remembered again how awfully the corpse had stunk, and the odor of filth which surrounded the beggar became to her nostrils the odor of corruption. A deep unholy terror possessed her. This was not Niels returned to explain the corpse, but the corpse of Niels returned to harry the soul of old Vibeke. She sat very still for fear that her fear would cross the small intervening space to the living corpse and that he would know his power over her. Little by little she forced her fear of him back, but only by the power of a greater fear, that he should know she feared him. She thought that if he talked, he would have less time to think of what harm he might do. She felt also that she would be less frightened if she spoke. So she began:

"That must have been a dreadful battle when you lost your arm."

"Aye," he said.

"And a long time ago. Fourteen years you have been doing without that arm."

"So long?" he said. "I hadn't counted."

"I cannot write but I can reckon," said Vibeke. "Fourteen years of begging. And all that time you never once came near Jutland?"

"As I told you," he said.

"Nor met a Jutlander?"

"Mistress Vibeke," said the beggar, "you ask me questions. Parson asks me questions. Master Thorwaldsen will ask more questions. I can wait until Parson and Magistrate come back, and answer them all at once."

Vibeke gave a short laugh.

"No doubt but you are a Jutlander, whatever else," she said.

The beggar lifted his shoulders, let them drop in a slow shrug.

"I answer questions. You do not believe me. Why do I waste my breath?"

There was justice in the remark, so that Vibeke did not reply. They sat, one on each side of the fire, in silence, while Vibeke's fear grew larger and pressed against her heart, as she said to herself, like an indigestion. Presently the beggar said:

"As you know something about it, how would you reckon Morten's wealth?"

"In money, I would not know," said the old woman. "In land, he had more than when he was born."

"You are a Jutlander also," said the beggar.

"But I know this," said she. "The one that inherits the wealth will inherit no good will with it."

Again the beggar lifted his shoulders in that sluggish gesture of unconcern.

"Who has wealth needs no good will," he said.

"Never believe that," said the old woman.

The beggar made no answer, and they waited, Vibeke never taking her eyes from the figure across from her, the beggar now and again stealing a covert glance at the old woman from beneath his heavy slanting brows. The time went slowly. Only once again did the beggar open his lips.

49

"Yet how should Master Thorwaldsen know Niels?" he said. "How many times did he meet Niels on the road, or at the market, and stop to speak with him? I shall ask for Anna Sörensdaughter, I shall."

Vibeke pressed her old lips more firmly together. The beggar continued to stare into the fire. Not for the world would she let him know what tenderness, what sense of loss the mention of that name brought into this hour of fear and dislike. She closed her eyelids slowly to press away the tears that gathered; opened them again upon a blurred figure in the firelight.

The coming of Judge Tryg Thorwaldsen and Pastor Juste changed all this. An eddy of damp air entered with them and made the chimney smoke. Vibeke ran to take the judge's cloak, to help the pastor off with his boots. At Thorwaldsen's command she drew up a trestle table to the middle of the floor, set chairs, brought candles, replenished the fire. The low roof seemed lower still because of the height of Thorwaldsen's figure, and the room smaller because of the shift of furniture.

"We will have light," said the judge, "so that I can look well at this man. And, Pastor, fetch your paper and ink. We will have a record of all that is said. Sit here by the table, Pastor. Vibeke, set the lights here."

The door being shut, the chimney drew properly again. The air cleared. The candle flames steadied themselves. Vibeke brought a pewter mug of beer and set it by the fire to warm for Judge Tryg Thorwaldsen. They began with the examination.

"It is established," said Pastor Juste, "that we have here a man who declares himself to be Niels, the brother of Morten Bruus, lately of Ingvorstrup in the parish of Vejlby. He further deposes that he left the province of Jutland in nutting time in the autumn before the defeat of King Christian, whom God save, at Lutter-am-Barenberge. That would have been, then, shall we say, in October 1625?"

The judge nodded. "As you say, Pastor Juste." The beggar also assented.

"Then, having been a soldier for seven years, off and on, he lost an arm at Lützen, and that would be in 1632."

Again Tryg nodded and the beggar copied him.

"He then begged his bread throughout the German duchies, as also in Bohemia and in Slesvig-Holstein, for the space of fourteen years. He is now returned to Aalsö parish in the month of November, and the year 1646, to lay claim to the fortune of his brother Morten. He has as yet called upon no one living and able to identify him."

"Write that all down," said Tryg, and after a pause the pastor answered, "It is written."

"And now, Master Thorwaldsen," said the beggar, "do you not remember Niels Bruus?"

"You could be Niels," said Thorwaldsen. "Or you could not be. I was present when they buried the body of Niels—so called."

The beggar grinned at that, and Tryg said, "I hope that you understand that it is a serious matter for you to represent yourself as someone other than

51

you are. You stand in the way of a heavy penalty if you should fail to prove yourself Niels Bruus."

"Anna Sörensdaughter will identify me," said the beggar with confidence.

The judge looked at him for a long moment without stirring, almost as if he had not spoken. Then he said, "Let me question you a little. You have asked us to remember Niels. If you are Niels, you will remember something of Vejlby, and of Aalsö. You were a boy here. Did you do your catechism with Pastor Qvist?"

The beggar shook his head. "With Pastor Peder Korf," he said, and added piously, "I did it none too well, more's the pity."

"But why not with Pastor Sören?" inquired the judge. "You were of his parish."

The beggar shrugged his shoulders. "We were none too good friends with Pastor Sören when I was a boy. Morten had quarrels with him, and Morten sent me to Pastor Korf. I did not always come when I was sent."

The judge considered this awhile and then said, "You must have known Vejlby well, however. Tell me something of Vejlby. The inn there—tell me, what was the name of the inn at Vejlby and where did it stand?"

"That is easy," said the beggar. "Everyone knows that the name of the inn was the Red Horse, and it stood on the market street, facing the east."

Juste Pedersen was about to interrupt, when Tryg checked him with a motion of his hand.

"Was there anything else you can remember about the Red Horse Inn?" he inquired.

The beggar had a faint smile. "It was also called the Sign of the Three-legged Horse," he said.

"He is wrong enough there," said Pastor Juste, "but he has probably been at a great many inns in his day, and perhaps we should not reckon this too seriously."

"But he is not wrong," said the judge. "When the Germans came, they burned the inn, and the new inn stands, as you are thinking, in quite another spot and has another name, but the old inn stood, as he says, on the market street facing east, and the artist who made the sign, for reasons of his own, painted the red horse with three legs." He reached into his pocket for a white linen handkerchief and wiped his hands upon it nervously. "In a horse-trading country, Pastor Juste, you will grant that even the churls remember a horse with three legs. But your memory is not always so clear," he said, turning again to the beggar, "and one thing else puzzles me. Why have you not asked Vibeke Andersdaughter to identify you?"

"Ah, she," said the beggar. "I have been a long time trying to remember her name. I know now. She was Pastor Sören's housekeeper in the old days. She has changed. She is old now. Besides, I never paid much attention to her."

Tryg looked at Vibeke. She answered slowly, "He might be Niels Bruus. I think he is Niels Bruus."

"Well, am I not Niels Bruus now?" demanded the beggar. "You say so—Vibeke says so."

"There is nothing so far," said Tryg very slowly, "to prove that you are *not* Niels Bruus. The whole matter now lies in how honest an explanation you can give . . ." He paused, and the beggar took the words out of his mouth.

"Of the corpse in the garden, eh? Well, I will tell you."

"Speak a little slowly," said Juste. "I cannot write too fast."

"Well," said the beggar, "as you know, I was a servant to Pastor Sören Qvist."

"Tell me," said Tryg curiously, "you that left Jutland because you were afraid of Morten, were you never afraid of Pastor Sören?"

"Oh no," said the beggar promptly. "The pastor was a good man. Even when he was angry, and struck me, I was not afraid of him, for he was still a good man. But Morten—Morten had always a kind of devil in him. Even when we were children I was always afraid of him. He was always much cleverer than I. He was older, too, and more handsome, but he was always cleverer. And always I did what he told me to. So when he told me to plague the pastor and make him angry, I did. Then Morten rewarded me. Morten did not love the pastor. Do you understand?"

"I begin to understand," said Thorwaldsen. "Go on."

"Then one day I made Pastor angry and he knocked me down. I remember it was nutting time. I ran home to Morten and told him what had happened, and he praised me and gave me good food. Then he locked me up. I thought that was strange, but Morten was cleverer than I. Master Thorwaldsen, cannot I have one swig from your mug? It makes me thirsty to talk so much."

Chapter Four

The judge swore under his breath, but pushed the pewter mug toward the beggar, who drank, and drank again. Finally he set the mug on the table, wiped his mouth with the sleeve of his crimson doublet, and went on with his story.

"Morten locked me up until midnight. This was at Ingvorstrup. Then he came, and he gave me a spade to carry. We went out toward Revn, and beyond, as well as I could tell, but we stopped at a crossroads. There was a suicide buried, not many days before. Morten said dig, and I dug, but Morten pulled the body out of the ground. I was frightened. I had not been a soldier then. I was not used to such things. Neither had the suicide been exorcised." He shuddered, and Vibeke crossed herself.

"We made the earth smooth again, and tramped on it to make it just as it had been. He hid the body in a beechwood, and we went back to Ingvorstrup. The sky was already getting light when we reached home. Then Morten locked me up again. The next night he came and fetched me, and took me to the beechwood. There he made me undress. Then he undressed the corpse. I tell you, I was frightened, and I asked him what he thought he was going to do, and he told me he was going to play a little trick on Pastor Sören, and that I should ask no more questions. Then he made me dress in the clothes of the suicide. That I did not like. And he dressed the body in my clothes, with everything I had been wearing, even to my earring. I had only one earring. Even that he took.

"Then he struck the dead man in the face with the

55

spade two or three times, and once on the crown of the head, and he said, laughing, 'That is to make him look more like you.' Then he put the body in a sack that he had brought with him, and he said to me, 'Carry the sack.' 'No,' I said, but I had to carry it all the same."

The beggar paused and looked into the mug, which was empty, and no one offered to refill it.

"I had to carry the sack all the way to Vejlby to the road that runs east of the pastor's garden to Tolstrup. I tell you, it was heavy. But Morten carried the spade. There we went into the wood that is on the hillside overlooking the garden, and we waited, and watched the road and the parsonage for some time. It was moonlight and we could see very well. But everything was still. No one came on the road. By and by Morten said to me, 'Go down to the house, to Parson's room, and bring me back his nightcap and his dressing gown.' But that he did not make me do. I was too frightened. I should have fallen on my knees before the hedge if I had tried to do that.

"Then Morten said, 'I will go myself,' and he left me, with the sack alone in the woods. I swear to you, I wished that I had never seen my brother Morten. I cursed him and I cursed the hour. But he came back after a little while, and he was wearing the dressing gown and the nightcap, and never a cat had heard him. He was clever, oh, he was. He reached into his pocket, then, and took out a little leather bag. I heard it go clink.

"He untied the bag, and he poured out on the

ground a little pile of silver. No, a big pile of silver. I had never seen so much money all at once before—no, nor since. Then he made me hold the bag, and he counted the money back into it, a piece at a time. There were one hundred rix-dollars. The moonlight came through the leaves and shone on every piece, so that he knew I could see that they were all good.

"He said, 'I am going to play a little trick on Pastor Sören, and you talk too much. You must go out of Jutland. I will give you that bag which you hold in your hands, but if you ever so much as show your nose in Jutland again, I will say that you stole the money, and have you hanged for it. Go now, and remember, my word against yours, and I am much cleverer than you.' Such a brother he was.

"I went that night as far as I could. I slept by day, and traveled by night, until I was in South Jutland. At first it was not so bad. When the money was gone, I joined with Wallenstein. After I lost my arm it was worse. I have had a bad time of it, all told, but now I shall be rich. He laughs best who lives longest, eh? This time I am cleverer than Morten, for I am still alive." He looked again into the pewter mug, then turned it upside down upon the table and waited, grinning hopefully.

Vibeke had not taken her eyes from the face of the one-armed man during this long recital. He had spoken with a slowness which in its way testified to his honesty, for he seemed never to have made this speech before. Indeed, it might have been surmised that he had avoided the subject even in his thought, turning his back upon it whenever it had edged into his conscious vision. When he had finished speaking, she stared at him unmoving for a long full minute and then dropped her face into her hands and began to weep. She wept as women do who have restrained their tears for a long time. She wept as if her heart would break. Judge Thorwaldsen also dropped his head in his hands, as if struck with a mighty contrition. Only Pastor Juste, whose head had been bent above his paper, laid down his quill, lifted his head, and, leaning back in his chair, stared at the beggar with eyes unclouded by sorrow but so intent that they might have run him through with their sharp light. The beggar, looking in surprise from the bowed head of the magistrate to the shielded face of Vibeke, brought back his eyes to the eyes of Juste, but could not sustain the narrowed steady gaze. His eyes faltered, turned aside; he sat looking at the floor. Suddenly Pastor Juste slapped his hand upon the table. He cried:

"But this man is a murderer!"

"Oh no," said the beggar, looking up quickly. "The corpse was a suicide. I swear to you it was a suicide. We never killed it."

"Fool, fool," said Juste, "the suicide is of no importance. This man is the murderer of Sören Qvist."

The beggar actually stood up at this, then, his knees giving way, sank slowly back upon his stool. "No, Pastor, no!" he said. "Morten never touched Pastor Sören. Nor I, neither. Pastor was sleeping in his bed. Morten only took the dressing gown."

"Is it conceivable," said Judge Thorwaldsen, lifting his bowed head from his hands and showing to the beggar a face so pale and strained that the man was frightened before he heard Tryg's words, "is it possible that you do not understand what befell Pastor Sören because of Morten's little trick with the corpse?"

"He was going to frighten Pastor, that was all," said the beggar.

"Oh, fool, fool," said Thorwaldsen, like Juste. "Morten buried the corpse in the garden. Then Morten accused the pastor of your death, and Pastor Sören Qvist was, God forgive us all, convicted of your murder and executed for it."

His words and the anguish in his voice had an appalling effect upon the beggar. He fell upon his knees, struck his breast with his one hand, then clutched at the table's edge as he fell forward, like a drowning man.

"But I did not kill Parson," he cried. "I never thought to kill him. Morten said it was just a trick. I am not a murderer. I would never have tried to kill him. Master Tryg, Master Tryg, protect me. I am not a murderer."

"Get up," said Thorwaldsen with iron in his voice. "Sit there on your stool, and be still."

The beggar let go of the table and fell to the floor, his hand before his face, crouching at the feet of the judge and shaking violently.

"Get up," said Tryg.

Still shaking, and slavering with terror so that the spittle ran down into the black stubble of his chin, the beggar rose slowly to his knees, then crept to his stool

59

and sat there, his arm clasped about his knees, his head bent, but his little, terrified eyes still fastened upon the judge from beneath his heavy brows.

Tryg said to Juste, "It is true that this man is not the murderer of Sören Qvist. The murderer of Pastor Sören died rich, and in his own bed. This man is the tool, the spade, the damned soul, he is indeed the dead and mindless body that was used against his master. What becomes of him is not half so much my concern as how to clear the name of Sören Qvist from this black shadow."

It was now Vibeke's turn to exclaim. She said, "I knew all along that there was something strange about the corpse. Indeed, I thought it was something bewitched. If not a cat, then a wax baby, such as the Swedes buried before Kalmar to bring disaster on the King's men. But if it was only an honest corpse, but the wrong man, then the witchcraft was elsewhere. Indeed and indeed, there must have been a spell upon the pastor. Indeed, I'm sure there was. He never let me bring the flying rowan into his room."

Tryg Thorwaldsen moved his right hand gently back and forth in a slow gesture of negation. "No," he said softly, "no, there was no spell upon the parson."

"But why," began the beggar, who had sat quietly through these two speeches, shaking only intermittently, like a man in the grip of a heavy chill, "why," he repeated, "did Parson let them kill him? He knew quite well that he did not murder me."

Chapter 5

The man who painted the sign of the Red Horse Inn at Vejlby was a realist rather than a theorist. He painted what he saw, like an artist, rather than what he knew, like a child or a farmer. Therefore the red horse of the sign stood with his forelegs close together, one obscuring the other, and his hind legs properly apart, as had stood the model for the sign. It was something of a joke in the surrounding country, but the painter had long since gone his wandering way, and even had he been at hand when the criticism began to accumulate, the owner of the inn would not have cared to spend more money to add another leg to his horse.

"Call it the Three-legged Horse if you like," he said to the customers who commented adversely upon the painter's work. "It serves as a sign either way, and the drinks are as good under a Three-legged Horse as a Red one."

He made the remark patiently once again on May Eve, 1625, to Niels Bruus, a young man in a peasant's blouse and short leather breeches, who was loafing in the taproom by the open window. Although Niels had a nose that was pointed and foxlike, his mouth was wide and rather foolishly good-natured. He had hit upon the joke of the three-legged horse a year since and had never let it go. The innkeeper knew that Niels was slow in the head and was forbearing.

"Aye, the drinks are good," said Niels. "Trust me for one more. You can always get the money out of Morten, if not out of me."

"In a fine way I can get the money out of Morten," said the innkeeper. "Neither will you get anything out of him but a cuff on the ear, if you don't begin to move. He's waiting for you this quarter hour to bring him round his horse."

"He works me like a servant, just because I'm his brother," said Niels, but he took the innkeeper's warning and went out by the back door into the innyard. Morten's horse was there, a big bay mare with which Niels was on the best of terms. It irked him that Morten owned her and that he almost never had the chance to ride her himself. She put her head down and nibbled at his shoulder with her lips while he adjusted her bridle. He checked the girth and refastened the buckle above a stirrup, and led her across the innyard to the market street, where, under the sign of the Red Horse, his brother Morten waited for him. Slighter and darker than Niels, older and better dressed, Morten Bruus resembled his brother so strongly that the most casual observer would have guessed the relationship. The brow was narrow and high, the nose pointed, with a curiously long and narrow nostril, but the mouth, unlike that of Niels, was fine-lipped and sensuously curved, and the expression of the eyes was far more penetrating. It was natural that Niels should be the one to hold the bridle and Morten the one to mount; but as Morten put his foot into the stirrup and took the reins from his brother, Niels, dropping behind him, gave the mare a resounding slap on the rump, which caused the mare to start suddenly to one side and left Morten precariously off balance, standing in one stirrup and clutching at the mane with both hands. It was as awkward a mounting as a man could have made. Niels guffawed, and the sudden heavy sound of his laughter was echoed, as Morten swung his leg over the mare's back and settled himself in the saddle, by a laugh as light and sharp and clear as the falling and breaking of a thin sheet of ice from a steep roof under the first heat of the sun. Morten twisted in the saddle to see whence came this springlike, crystal sound.

A girl had come out of the door across the street from the inn, and stood, still on the threshold, with the door closed behind her. Against the blackened oak, with the western sunlight full upon her, no figure that Morten had ever seen had been so brilliant. Small and slender, unlike the girls of the peasantry, she stood with the woolen overskirt of bright green tucked up thickly about her hips, the clear yellow of the camlet underskirt showing from the knee down. Her russet bodice, tight about her breast, let show the sleeves of green, with puffs of white linen. White-skinned, with a whiteness no sun could darken, but only gild, above the crisp white collar shone the laughing face, under

63

the cap of crisp and flaunting white, framed by a line of red-gold hair; and Morten was so near to her, in the narrow street, that the golden hazel of her eyes was as distinct as the colors of her garments. He looked her over without shame, from the top of her cap to her bare white ankles and the feet in the square-toed narrow leather shoes.

The girl bit her lip, and her face became hot. She should not have laughed, but it had happened so quickly that she had not had time to consider. Besides, she was happy and the laugh had been near the surface. No one but a clown, she thought, would have made such a spectacle of himself in mounting a horse, and a clown would not have been insulted by her laughter. But this man, although he wore the clothes of a well-to-do peasant, was without servility. He did not smile, he did not even lift an eyebrow, and he said nothing; but his look, going over her so deliberately, made her feel suddenly, in spite of all her heavy skirts and crisp linen, as naked as her ankles. She stepped down the one step to the hard beaten earth of the street and, checking herself lest she seem to move hastily, turned a shoulder to him and walked straightly away. Morten watched her until she passed out of sight. Then he said to Niels, "Who was the wench?"

Niels, half in mockery and half in surprise, answered, "Would you not know?"

"Who was she?" repeated Morten, without a flicker of graciousness.

"Who but Anna Sörensdaughter," said Niels.

"The pastor's daughter?" said Morten.

Chapter Five

"Who else," said Niels.

"Pastor and I are old acquaintances," said Morten nastily, "but I have not met his daughter." He kicked his horse and started off in a direction opposite to that which the girl had taken. When he had gone a short distance he called over his shoulder to Niels, "Are you coming along home?"

"Not I," said Niels. "I stay for the fires." And, feeling easier as the distance between him and his brother increased, he touched his forelock mockingly, spun round on his heel, and ducked back into the courtyard of the inn.

Anna Sörensdaughter took the long way home. There had been but a delicate warmth in this last day of April, barely enough to last over into the evening as the wind from the west rose gently and intermittently. In the grainfields there were but fine sharp spears of green, and in the beechwoods only the first unfurling of leaves. The great old oaks which stood one in each field throughout the plowed manor land were ever so faintly brushed with watery green. From amid the green transparent crowns of lindens the steep thatched roofs of farm buildings threw down their bluish shadows, lengthening toward the east, and every little granite pebble on the sandy roadway cast also its long shadow on the bright earth. The air flowed about the girl's ankles almost as cold as the water in the small streams and touched her bare arms and her forehead pleasantly, and the contrast between the touch of the wind and the brightness of the evening sunlight delighted her.

The Trial of Sören Qvist

There were swarms of small flies dancing in the air, the quick flight of small rusty-headed birds across the road, the notes of the lark dropping from the sky, all the texture of the air interwoven with the sounds of life; and there were also the far-off lowings of the cattle, and the sound of a violin and a tuba, intermittent, like the evening wind, as Anna drew nearer to a little knoll not far from the road. She remembered unwillingly, as she went, and chided herself again for her stupidity, her laughter at the awkwardness of the man on the bay mare. His look, which she remembered all too sharply, she interpreted as evil. Yet she walked with a wonderful lightness and awareness in all her body, as if her blood ran quicker, her hearing were more acute, her eyes more swift and clear than usual. It was as if she had been startled awake, as, after moments of sudden and temporary fear, or of brief anger, the body seems to have leaped into a quickened state of being. But she, strangely enough, had passed from a moment of shame into a state of exquisite vitality. It was May Eve. That she remembered well, and that strange things were known to come to pass before the midnight. So she went forward lightly, on the brink of a joyous anticipation.

At the knoll the men were stacking wood for the fire.

"When do you light it?" she called.

"As soon as it grows a little dark, mistress," one answered.

She watched them for a few moments, recognizing Hans from the Vejlby parsonage, the stableboy from the manor, the shoemaker's boy from the village. As she was about to proceed on her way, she met three women coming arm in arm. The one in the middle, a soft-cheeked woman with round blue eyes, halted the other two with a pressure of her arms.

"You should stay for the dancing, Mistress Anna," she said.

"Vibeke, you are too early," the girl answered. "They haven't yet stacked all the wood."

"I can help them a little then," said Vibeke, "with my tongue."

"Hans is there," said the girl. "The others?"

"They'll be along soon enough," said Vibeke. "Parson let them go early."

"Well, have a good time," said the girl, and, as she passed them, "I might come back later."

A little farther on she passed the musicians, who were carrying their instruments for the time being in silence. She exchanged greetings with them, and when she had gone another hundred yards or so, she heard them tuning up again. They had reached the knoll. She passed one other person as she neared the parsonage—Kirsten, the girl who helped with the dairy. Her long flaxen hair was in braids, she wore a new red skirt, and the pointed wooden shoes on her feet were gay with painted flowers. Shyly she greeted Anna, who clapped her hands to see her friend so fine.

Vejlby parsonage, when Anna reached it, seemed as deserted as on a Sunday morning. Yet even in desertion it had a welcoming and generous air. It also had its cloudily piled treetops about the peaked gables. Beyond the hazy green the plastered walls were white as snow.

The farm buildings were grouped in an open square, the barn and byre to the west, the salthouse and dairy to the north. On the southern side of the courtyard, and facing north, the long rectangle of the dwelling house under the steep golden thatch presented two doors, one the door to the servants' quarters, the other, and more important, to the kitchen. The house had originally consisted of only these two rooms. When the parson brought home his bride, a new part, which contained two rooms and a passageway, had been added on the western end so that the old and new together formed an ell enclosing a garden open to the east and south, for, as the parson said, the morning sunlight is good for all growing things, and the south gives the needed warmth in this cold climate. The garden was sheltered also from the western wind, which was sometimes too bitter in the fall, and from the western sun, which sometimes shone too fiercely in the summer afternoons. He had hedged the garden with hazel and box, and since it was easy of access from his own room, in the new part, he made it his special province, and few people labored in it save himself. The new part contained two rooms, reached from a passage on the garden side of the kitchen. No door was hung at the kitchen entrance to the passageway, but there were good doors at the opening of the parson's room into the passage, and from the Bride's Room. Thus all visitors to the parson entered first at the kitchen and passed the scrutiny of Vibeke, while the pastor could, when tired by his studies or his thoughts, escape into his sheltered garden.

Anna crossed the courtyard and pushed the door to the kitchen. It was not locked. It was never locked. There was no lock on any door in the place. A big dog with a broad head and a heavy ruff of brown fur rose from beside the doorstep and wagged his tail and then lay down again. Anna stood on the threshold and looked within, and saw and heard no one. On the other side of the courtyard, by the dairy, a white cat and a three-colored cat were washing their paws. They watched the girl without interrupting their own activity. The shadow of the byre fell long across the yard almost beyond the rich pile of manure, and the wide doorway was dark. Anna could not see within, but she caught the sound of her father's voice.

At the door to the byre she heard the voice more plainly, although she still could not see the parson.

"Gently there, my girl," said the parson from within one of the stalls. "Time does it, time and the kindness of God."

Three cautious white hens came jerkily through the doorway and hesitated, looking, with little stretches of their necks, down the aisle between the stalls.

"Are you talking to me?" called the girl into the long room.

The parson answered with a laugh, which was interrupted by a long, lowing groan.

"Golden Rose, the beautiful," he called, "is by way of giving us a calf."

"Oh," said Anna. "I will change my shoes and come help you."

"There is no hurry," called the parson in a tranquil voice.

In the Bride's Room, Anna Sörensdaughter smiled to herself as she unfastened her broad collar and laid it carefully in a chest, took off her leather shoes, dusted them, and set them beside the collar. The Bride's Room, unlike the kitchen, had been ceiled, and the top of the big bed reached almost the beams. There was little in the way of furniture in the room save the opened chest, and another like it, and the great bed, but the chests were both finely carved, and the bedposts also, for they had been a part of her mother's dowry. Her mother had died when Anna was small. The parson now slept on a pallet in his study, and Anna inhabited the Bride's Room alone.

She took off the cap of flaring holland, working with little quick angular gestures, and tied on a dull blue cap that fastened close about her hair with a puckering string. She put on an apron to protect her holiday skirts, slipped her bare feet into a pair of wooden shoes. Then she returned to the byre. The dog followed her to the doorway. The white hens had flown up into the baskets hung by the stalls and were settling themselves for the night with much rustling of feathers and sleepy inquiries. In the farthest stall the parson knelt on one knee by a leggy little creature in the straw.

"Another red one," he said, "as truly as the apple grows on the tree. Fetch me a rushlight, my darling, and let us see if she wears the white star."

70

Chapter Five

The star was there, and the parson was pleased. The Golden Rose, though tired, was contented too. The rushlight flared uncertainly upon the silver-satiny coat and the questioning eye of the newborn, and on the watchful eye of its mother, catching the roundness and brightness of the eyes like jewels out of the shadow. Then the parson snuffed it between his thumb and forefinger and, with his hand on his daughter's shoulder, said: "The little one has a coat the color of your hair. But it will darken. Well, and I did not look for you home so early. I thought you would be dancing all the evening."

"Tryg is so solemn," she answered. "He says that the dancing is for the peasantry. I could not persuade him to stay. He went back to Rosmos alone. And Vibeke said that you were alone. So I came home."

"You are a good girl," he said fondly as they proceeded to the house. "The dancing is good for them. They work very hard, poor souls. What if they dance until they fall down and have to be carried to one side? It is as good for them as drinking much beer, until they fall down; and the King's physicians have advised that for the good of the body. The dancing purges the animal spirits and lightens the heart, as the drinking purges the animal body."

"Vibeke will surely dance until she falls down," said the girl.

They entered the kitchen. The parson said, "I milked before you came, good luck. Do you find us some bread, and I will bring in the milk, and we will have a bite together—unless, that is, you are too stuffed with dainties to be hungry."

"I should like a cup of milk," said Anna.

She brought a woven willow basket full of small brown loaves, each with three little peaks or corners on the top, and two beechwood mugs bound in silver and having handles of silver. The pastor brought a red earthen pitcher, full of the evening's milk, still faintly warm and sweet-smelling.

"Let us sit on the doorstep," he said. "It is a little chill and dark within, and also it smells very strongly of rue."

"I don't like it either," she said, "the smell of rue. And there is not enough rosemary to cover it up. But Vibeke would not be happy if she were not allowed to sprinkle all the kitchen with it before May Eve. She says it will keep the witches away. Do you believe that?"

The parson filled the two cups before he answered. The dog lay down with his head against the parson's foot. "Beech is the best wood," the parson remarked. "It gives no taste to the milk. As for the rue, I think we do not need it against the witches, but it serves to keep the fleas down."

The parson took a long draught of milk and wiped his mustache, parting it with his fingers. The thick white hair and full beard had once been as golden a red as his daughter's hair, but the color had been transmuted with time, until now there was hardly a trace of the red in hair or beard. The hair was crisp, rather than silky, and inclined to twine itself in small ringlets. The parson was a big man. Standing, he must have measured well over six feet, and he was broad in proportion. He wore the leather breeches and loose blouse of the peasantry, the yellow cloth stockings and wooden shoes. The hand which held the beechwood mug was callused and stained, and there was no task about the farm for which it was not sufficiently strong and skillful.

"Vibeke does lots of things that no one else bothers about," said Anna, holding her mug with two hands like a child. "She washes her hands every morning of her life. She says it is because witches are foul and dread everything clean, and that washing the hands is as good as a charm against them."

"Well, that is to be praised," said the parson.

"She stole a bit of wax from the Easter candle, did you know? And made a little cross and set it in the thatch above the door by which the cattle and horses come in."

The parson smiled. "Yes, I knew it," he said.

"And she says that tonight the witches will be flying overhead to go to a great meeting in Skaane, and trolls will come out of the mounds in the heath. That is why she sprinkled the kitchen with rosemary and rue. She is dreadfully afraid of witches."

"She has her reasons, doubtless," said the parson. "Yes, she has her reasons."

"But do you think the witches are so greatly to be dreaded?"

"I think that they are given credit for far greater ill than they are capable of," said the parson.

"Well, but do you think," persisted his daughter, "that they will be flying overhead to Skaane tonight? And is Sweden more full of witches than Denmark?"

The parson laughed at the second question. "Sweden is great for witches," he answered, "but Germany is worse. But, soberly, it is possible that Satan may transport the bodies of the witches through the air, for it is written that Satan conveyed our Lord to the top of a mountain and from there showed him the kingdoms of the earth. But the dread of witches should be no greater than the dread of Satan, for surely you did not suppose that a witch by herself, or by himself, for there are men witches especially in Germany, could accomplish anything of power? If a witch shakes water from a horse's tail over his left shoulder, and thereby brings a storm to pass, it is neither the witch nor the water that caused the storm, but the devil, who takes the shaking of the horse's tail as a signal and a sign, and therewith accomplishes what he has covenanted with his servant to do. But the power of the devil is limited by God, and only such evil may he accomplish as God in his wisdom permits him."

The shadow of the byre had by now crept forward to encompass the entire courtyard. Anna looked up at the eastern sky, where, toward Skaane and behind the transparent crown of a great beech, the moon was rising. It was almost at the full and it shone as pale as winter butter.

"But then they can fly through the air," she said, "and pass through keyholes and bring a murrain on the cattle, and sour the cream in the jug."

Chapter Five

"I do not think they can pass through keyholes," said her father. "And if they bring a sickness on the cattle, or sour the cream, that hardly seems to me a matter for burning."

"But then Vibeke is right to be afraid of them?" said Anna.

"Vibeke has her reasons," said the parson, as he had said before, "but as for the rest of us, I see no reason to be more afraid of witches than of any of the other manifestations of the devil. And against the power of our Adversary," he continued, somewhat in the voice in which he spoke from Vejlby church pulpit, "there availeth nothing so much as the upright heart and the busy hand. I do not grant that the cross of Easter wax, or the dried rue or rosemary or various other herbs, or much washing of the hands are more potent than these. The power of the Adversary is great, and at all times to be reckoned with, but the power of the Lord Jehovah is greater. I put my trust in the power of the Lord."

In the byre the cattle stirred and a horse whinnied, noises near and yet muffled. The parson, leaning forward, his elbows on his knees, looked into the spring twilight as if he were reading a book. This was a matter to which he had given much thought. He said again, "There has been too much fear of witches, and too much persecution of them for trivial offenses."

"It is not for such things as the souring of cream, then, that they burn them," his daughter interrupted, "but for their pact with the devil."

"It is the devil we should be afraid of," said the

pastor. "And as for those miserable and pitiable women, they should be reasoned with, and brought back to the church. For was not Peter himself forgiven who denied the Lord three times? I thank the Lord that in Denmark there is some moderation in these things. Here, under Christian, in spite of his wars, we have some Christian enlightenment, and not a terror as in those countries to the south of us. Yes, I praise Christian for a wise and liberal King. And if the King himself causes his own daughter to be baptized without exorcism, why should not I, his servant, continue to baptize infants in the same manner? Faith, I shall continue to do so," he added with warmth, "for all they can say, and no man shall make me believe that the innocent child fresh from the womb can be full of foul fiends."

"You make me remember," said Anna, "what I was bid to tell you. I had almost forgot with all this bother about witches. Ida Möller greets you, and asks will you church her and baptize her child—without exorcism, Father—on Whitsun?"

"Ah," said the parson, vastly pleased, "so the little one has made its entrance safe into this world."

"It is a little girl," said Anna, "and Ida is happy for the child and sad for her man."

The parson sighed. "It is a sorry business," he said.

"I wish that we might help her," said Anna, her eyes filling with distress at the remembrance.

"I hope we may," her father answered. "Well, child, I have yet to write a sermon for the week, but you have given me a good start on it. Are you going to bed?"

Anna looked at the moon. There were shadows as of leaves upon its face.

"I think I'll walk a little way down the lane," she replied. "The night is so pretty."

The parson rose to his feet, taking the two mugs in one hand and the pitcher in the other. He leaned over to kiss his daughter on the cheek. "God go with you," he said, and went into the house.

Anna went down the lane, and the moon went with her, drawing clear of the trees and shining more silverly. She heard a splashing in the duckpond. The ducks and the geese were excited by the moonlight. She heard very faintly the sound of the violins and the tuba. She went a little farther, breathing the sweet cold freshness of the air, wondering if she should not do better to go home and to bed, but, like the ducks and geese, she felt awakened by the moonlight on the newly sprouting fields. As she went farther the music became clearer until she could catch the tune. They were playing the "Little Man in a Fix." Then all at once she took off her apron, rolled it into a bundle and hid it under a bush, straightened her skirts, undid the blue cap and smoothed her hair, and began to run toward the music.

On a morning shortly before Whitsun, Parson Sören Jensen Qvist was seated in his study. This room, like that in which the bride bed stood, was ceiled. It had one small window, unglazed, to be closed with a wooden shutter, and one door which opened on the passage to the kitchen and the garden. The door was closed this morning, for the parson wished to be uninterrupted. The window was open, and through it came the rustle of leaves, for in the week or more elapsing since May Eve, when the boughs stood veiled in the faintest green, the leaves had spread themselves, silken and full, and as the parson sat before his books he reflected that this was the first day since the last autumn when he had been aware of their murmuring.

The parson's library was more ample than that of most of his contemporaries in the country. He had brought from his student days at Leipsic and at Copenhagen not only the Bible in the Danish translation of Christian Pedersen and the Bishop Palladius, and Luther's Catechism, the mainstay and absolute necessity of his calling, but also the hymns and sermons of Hans Tausen, Bishop of Ribe. Beside these stood a play, the *Miserly Miscreant*, admitted to this company of books chiefly because the author, Justesen Ranch, was also the priest at Viborg. Next to that stood the New Testament in Greek, and a collection of works by pagan Greek philosophers, much read. Dying unilluminated before the birth of our Lord, these had undoubtedly bequeathed their souls to Limbo, as in the representation by the great Italian poet, but their words were still full of excellent wisdom, and Sören Qvist held them in affection and veneration.

In his student days he had built for himself a chest with pigeonholes—a dovecote for his books, he called it—and a lid that could be let down and used as a writing table. This chest still housed his library and his sermons, his pen and ink and dish of fine sand, and was seldom closed. He had before him that morning the happy task of choosing a text for the Whitsun sermon, for, although he admired the sermons of Bishop Tausen, he seldom used them, but took pleasure in composing his own. His talk with Anna had led him to reread the Book of Job, and he had considered preaching on the power of evil as limited by the power of God, but then, remembering Ascension Day, had preached instead on that subject, taking his text from Luke, and telling his parishioners, for they were simple folk, of the travelers to Emmaus, and of the revelation in the breaking of bread, and of the broiled fish and the honeycomb, and the parting at Bethany, and so to the instruction of repentance, dwelling more upon the promised forgiveness than upon the sin, for he felt a great tenderness for the hard-working folk who assembled in his church. He still wished to preach from the text in Job, and thought that this might be the time. He opened his Bible and drew forth the Catechism.

There lay, among other papers in his desk, one on which he had made notes at some other time, and he drew that forth too, idly, for he had forgotten on what subject he had made the notes. Because of his forgetfulness, it seemed to him, as he read the words which he had once written, that here was an instruction from God that he should choose his text from one of these which he had searched out and set down on an earlier day. As his hand lay upon the paper, the sheet seemed to have become an instrument of the will of God, and before he had read every word he was filled with an emotion like that with which he had set them down, yet a little less sorrowful, a little more filled with humility, and touched with awe at this sense of divine interference. He read:

He that is slow to anger is better than the mighty; and he that ruleth his spirit than he that taketh a city. Proverbs, 16:32.

A soft answer turneth away wrath: but grievous words stir up anger. Proverbs, 15:1.

Be not hasty in thy spirit to be angry: for anger resteth in the bosom of fools. Ecclesiastes, 7:9.

For a bishop must be blameless, as the steward of God; not self-willed, not soon angry . . . no striker. Titus, 1:7.

Sören Qvist was not a bishop; he was only a country parson, but he was a servant of God, and, remembering such, he sat staring at the sheet of paper. The sound of leaves stirring in the May morning came to him remotely, and the sound of hoofbeats on the road. He heard the voices of his servants very far away and was unconcerned with them.

In the kitchen that morning Vibeke was mixing bread and Anna, with the help of Kirsten, was churning. The kitchen, although a moderately large room, was crowded. Many occupations had their place there. It had once held the whole life of the family, and the girls had brought their work there as much for sociability as that the warmth of the room might hasten the butter to come. Vibeke and Kirsten shared the bed in the alcove that had formerly been the parson's. Hans and any other men or boys who might be helping the parson slept in the smaller room to the east. At the western end of the kitchen the big hooded fireplace with raised hearth and closed brick oven took the middle third of the wall. On either side of the fireplace, in the alcoves formed by its big shoulders, were the spinning wheel, the reel, wooden chests, and a little table. In one of these alcoves, before the new part had been built, the parson had been used to keep his books, and it was still a corner in which a man might sit, a little withdrawn from the main current of activities, and drink a mug of beer in peace. The brown dog had taken refuge there, under the table, this morning, his chin on his paws, immobile, with bright watchful eyes.

A few chickens stepped through the opened doorway, looking for crumbs about the long trestle table where Vibeke was working. She clapped her floury hands at them to scare them away, and Kirsten, who was pouring cream into the churn, looked over her shoulder and laughed to see them scatter. In doing so, she spilled some cream, and the three-colored cat, white with patches of yellow and gray, with one yellow ear and one white, crept forward with lengthened steps to lap it up.

"If there is more cream today, we can use it," said Anna, peering into the opened churn. Kirsten bent beside her to see for herself how much was needed, and for a moment the two heads, capless this morning, one pale gold, one red gold, and bound with smooth braids, were together. Then Kirsten straightened and, swinging the empty pitcher, went out to the dairy. Someone on horseback came into the courtyard as the girl went out. Anna, listening, thought, "That is not one of ours," and heard the exchange of greetings, but not of words, as Kirsten went on. She pushed back her sleeves toward the shoulder, feeling warm, and stood, with hands resting lightly on the edge of the churn, waiting for Kirsten's return, and wondering, not too greatly, who the visitor might be. Whoever it was delayed to tie up his mount, and then the footsteps came leisurely toward the door. Anna did not at once recognize the man who presently stood in the doorway, for the light was all behind him, but as he stepped forward, she started, ever so little. It was the man who had looked at her so strangely on May Eve from the back of the bay mare.

He did not look at her now; he did not seem to see her, but advanced to Vibeke, and asked, in an oddly resonant voice, if the parson were at home. Vibeke said that he was. Her tone was not friendly.

"Then can I talk with him?" said the man.

"Well, but he is busy," said Vibeke. "He is in his study, and thinking about the Sunday preachment, and he does not like to be disturbed at such a time."

"The matter is pressing," said the man. Then, seeing that Vibeke was not convinced, he added, "It concerns a parishioner of his, the man Hans Möller who has but lately been sent to the King's shipyards."

"Oh," said Anna suddenly, "if it concerns Hans Möller, my father will want to see him, certainly."

The man turned at this and, with a great show of surprise and pleasure, bowed to her. Then he turned back to Vibeke.

"Well," said the housekeeper unwillingly, "that being that, I suppose I must risk disturbing him."

She dusted her hands on her apron and went down the passageway to Pastor Sören's room. The two in the kitchen heard her knock and enter the room and shut the door behind her.

The stranger then crossed the kitchen toward Anna.

"You are looking very pretty this morning," he said. "The opened blouse is more becoming than the collar, and"—his gaze dropping toward the floor—"the bare foot is prettier than the shoe. And blue becomes you."

She did not answer him, neither did she look away. He was taller than she had realized, almost as tall as her father, but not nearly so strongly built. She might have considered him handsome if she had not felt so great a distrust of him. His manner was seemingly as

83

pleasant as he could make it, and his voice discreet, and yet she was not sure that he was not insulting her. She pressed her fingers firmly against the damp cold wooden edge of the churn and said nothing, but the strangest feeling swept over her, an alarm that ebbed quickly, leaving a little tingling of fire in each fingertip.

Parson Sören Qvist heard the name of his visitor with surprise. The sheet of paper with its five scriptural warnings still lay under his hand, and as Vibeke shut the door firmly behind her and made her unwilling announcement, the parson felt that her message coincided oddly with his coming upon the unremembered sheet. He gave his instruction to have the visitor brought in. When Vibeke had left the two men, and Morten Bruus had himself shut the door upon the sound of her retreating footsteps, the parson was still sitting with his fingertips touching the edge of the sheet of paper.

The light in the room was very cool, although the outer world was flooded with brightness. Here the morning light penetrated only through the small window set deep in the wall, and was spread upon the whitewashed surfaces without contrast of sun or shade. The place was bare, almost as stern as a monastic cell, and the parson sat there unmoving, turned a little away from his chest of books and papers. The whiteness of his hair and beard and the breadth of the shoulders under the dark fustian coat gave him dignity, and there was in his expression, as his eyes met those of his visitor, a gravity, even more, an intentness of one considering a mystery, that made it difficult for Morten to

84

explain his errand. The parson did not speak to him, but simply nodded once, very slightly. Morten looked about for a chair and sat down, holding his hat before his knees. He was not used to being embarrassed, and he did not remain so long.

"I am of your parish, Pastor Sören, although I have had little dealing with your church."

The pastor seemed to acknowledge the truth of this without bothering to speak. Morten went on.

"Lately one of your people was convicted of stealing a sum of money from me and was sent to the King's shipyards."

Again the pastor waited for him to go on.

"It has come to me since that Mistress Anna Sörensdaughter is much distressed about the condition of this man's wife." Still the parson gave him no help, and he came to the point as quickly as he could. "Since it distresses her, and you, perhaps I could withdraw the charges against this fellow Möller, if you would make some guaranty for his more honest behavior in the future."

"It is too late," said the parson simply. "He has been judged, and sentenced. If the evidence was true, you may forgive him, but the law does not. If the evidence was false—are you willing to admit yourself a perjurer?"

"Well, hardly that," said Morten, smiling. "But, if I cannot have the charges withdrawn, I can perhaps lighten the burden for Ida Möller, who has been charged to repay me, in one way or another, for the full amount of the stolen money."

"For that," said the parson with the simplicity with which one speaks to a child, and with the reserve with which one may address an enemy, "for that you need hardly ask my permission. By all means forgive the poor woman the debt. And whenever that is done, be sure that I shall hear of it."

This was clearly the moment for Morten to take his departure, but he did not rise. Instead he looked down at his hat, twirled it a few times between his fingers, and then said, quite easily, "Pastor Sören, you and I have not been on the best terms in the world. I came to speak to you about Ida Möller in the hope that you might not think me such a bad sort as you have been in the habit of doing. You know that I am well off in the matter of lands and goods. With a little luck and some trying I might even turn out to be a good sort— so that even you might have a better opinion of me."

The pastor raised his hand as if in protest and then let it fall very softly, palm down, flat upon the paper on his desk. The impulse toward speech, whether in anger or agreement, which had been visible upon his face although he had never opened his lips, ebbed as visibly as if it had been a suffusion of blood. The man before him looked down at his hat again, gave it a little shake as if to dislodge a drop of water, and said, "I should be a fool if I did not realize that you have a very great influence in your parish, and in the neighboring parishes as well. I know that I myself have not a great reputation for charity. But I assure you, I am maligned. I am not nearly as hardhearted as they say. I have only insisted upon taking what was my own."

Chapter Six

"It is necessary," said the pastor with great mildness, "sometimes to give."

"Well, I will do that, with your help," said Morten Bruus.

"Very well," said the pastor patiently. "I will help you, if you need help."

"Also, I would wish . . ." Morten began. Then he stopped and laughed in an embarrassed manner. "I would wish, Pastor Sören, the help of your daughter Anna. In fact, Pastor Sören, I have come this morning chiefly to ask for the hand of your daughter in marriage."

The room was very still. Sören Qvist looked at his visitor and noted that he was dressed with unusual neatness and that his manner was respectful to the point of being obsequious. As the interview had begun he was not sure but that Morten Bruus had come to make fun of him. He had thought that he detected an element of mockery in the manner of Bruus, and only the touch of the sheet of paper beneath his hand had held his anger in check. The offer of marriage first struck the old man as further mockery. Then, for his eyes were keen, he detected an expression in those of Morten which seemed to vouch for his earnestness, at least in this one request. And as the realization grew in the mind of Sören Qvist that this man, whom he hated, was asking for the thing dearest to his heart, he heard in the intense stillness of the room a buzzing that increased to a dull roar, and he knew that it was the blood beating in his own ears.

Anger such as he had not experienced in a score of

years rose in him like a fire. A tremendous strength seemed to fill his arms, and the desire to use it was such that he felt his body would burst if he restrained it. He stood up and, with the greatest effort in the world, kept his hands from touching Morten Bruus. Morten stood up too. It was quite plain that the parson was not going to agree to his request. Indeed it was evident that he would be lucky to leave the room without having his head broken. He made a step sideways, forgetting, in his moment of panic, just where the door was.

Sören Qvist locked his arms behind him and made a step forward, then he turned and paced a few steps in the opposite direction, and finding that this striding back and forth did help him to hold his fury in control, he began a steady pacing, backward and forward, in front of Morten; yet he was too enraged and insulted to speak a word. Morten, in his nervousness, edged away from the path which the pastor was treading. He would have been only too glad to escape, but he presently found that his way to the door was cut off by the pastor's march. After a time he found himself standing behind the parson's chair, and something impelled him to look down at the parson's desk. Morten could read and his eye was quick. He saw the texts which the parson had been contemplating, and he suddenly realized to what he owed his temporary safety. He had heard stories of the parson's anger, as of his strength. And Morten was a coward. However, something reckless prompted him to twit the parson with his great weakness.

"I understand," he said softly, "to what I owe your unusual forbearance. I commend the last text to you, and also, particularly, the next to the last one."

The parson wheeled and confronted the mocking, slightly swaying figure of his enemy. If Morten Bruus had spat in the old man's face, he could not have insulted him more directly. There was no word upon that sheet of paper that was not as clear to the pastor's eye as if he had not just inscribed it, and his realization of Morten's implication was instant. All the patience and tolerance summoned with so great effort for the consideration of Morten's incomprehensible change of character vanished as in a silent explosion.

With a single cry the pastor reached for Morten Bruus, got a firm grip upon the shrinking body, slung it over his shoulder like a bundle of hay, and started down the passage on the run. He hardly noticed, as he charged through the kitchen, how the women scattered before him, Anna and Kirsten to one side, Vibeke to the other, overturning her mixing bowl in her haste. He reached the courtyard and there flung Morten to the ground. Standing over him briefly, he said, in a voice which could be heard from the kitchen to the byre, "Get out of my sight. Stay out of my sight. If ever I catch you on my land again, I'll flay you to the bone." He returned, through the kitchen, down the passageway to his study, and entered it, and closed the door upon himself and his anger.

No sooner did he feel himself alone than his anger disappeared. His bones seemed to turn to water, and a most awful sickness took possession of him. He sank to his knees, shaking, and covered his face with his hands. He had not felt so in years. This anger, which came upon him so suddenly and with such absolute power, had been the greatest trial of his life.

Memories rushed upon him. The face of a young German student, blond, arrogant, and opinionated, rose before him. He felt again the sword in his hand, and in his heart the furious desire which had possessed him to kill that young man. The reason for the quarrel escaped him. He remembered that he had thought the German no better than a Calvinist, and that he had seemed to him both blasphemous and personally insulting; that a duel had been arranged promptly, and that he had wished to kill. When it was over and the German was found to be merely wounded, not slain, Sören had taken himself to the edge of the meadow where the duel had taken place, and there had come over him such a revulsion of feeling that he was for an hour too weak to move.

He reflected then that God had saved him from becoming a murderer. He saw then how unfitting it was for two men who pretended to be servants of God, or who were at least studying for such a responsibility, to quarrel with each other. Yet he had wished to kill. God had saved him; he had not saved himself. Years after he understood that it was not because of the point of theology involved, but for the German's arrogance that he had wished to kill him, and he had thanked God for His intervention.

The habit of anger had been born with him, he thought, and, in general, he had indulged it only in violent speech, or upon inanimate objects. He had sometimes in his fury stood and torn a bridle to bits, to keep his hands from venting their anger upon the beast who had enraged him. But once, long ago, he had touched a living creature, and the memory of it had never quite left him. He was a little boy, strong for his age, and he had been sent to the hills to tend sheep. He had little enough in his package for dinner, and he was hungry enough to have eaten it before the sun was very high above the edges of the hills, but he remembered that the day would be long, and he had, with great forbearance for his years, hid the package of bread and cheese under a heather bush and under a rock. But the dog who was the co-tender of the flock had found the package, and, dragging it out, devoured every bit of it before the boy found him nosing in the kerchief in which everything had been tied.

In his hunger and disappointment he had beaten the dog, beaten him furiously, beaten him continuously, and finally hit him on the head with a rock, until the creature lay perfectly still. Then his anger left him, and he remembered that the dog was his friend, and he laid his head beside the furry head of the dog and caressed him and pleaded with him for forgiveness. But the dog was dead. The weakness and illness which he felt again in his old age he first felt then, as he lay in the sun-drenched heather, flat to the ground, in the greatest despair and shame of his young life. The sound of the sheep cropping the short grass between the bushes came to him, and the droning of bees in the waxy heather bells above his head. He smelled the sweetness of the stunted broom and of the earth itself which gave up a spicy fragrance under the heat, and all these things, instead of consoling him, became a part of the intense anguish of his despair. That he had been little and very hungry was some excuse to him as he looked back across the years, but to the child in the heather it had been no excuse, after his anger passed, because he had loved the dog. Upon the May morning when he had felt the full violence of his anger against Morten Bruus he might have excused himself in that he believed the man to be an enemy of his poor, but he could not excuse himself in any degree because he felt that God had warned him on that day. So the two moments of anguish melted together, across the years, and the man felt the despair of the boy because he also had betrayed a trust.

The parson did not leave his room for hours after. In the kitchen Vibeke picked up her wooden mixing bowl, picked up her partly kneaded dough and brushed the straw and specks of dirt from it. Anna and Kirsten stood together by the churn, too frightened to proceed at once with their work. Vibeke, glancing through the open door as she knelt for her dough, saw Morten Bruus lie still, then slowly roll over and get to his feet. He brushed the straw and dust from his shoulder and side, put on his hat, and, glancing only once toward the kitchen doorway, went slowly to his horse, untied it, and mounted. The three women in the kitchen heard him ride away, and it was not until the last sound of hoofs left the lane that Kirsten put out her hand to the dasher.

Chapter Six

"Ah," said Vibeke feelingly, "when I saw Morten Bruus come into this kitchen I said to myself, 'Here comes trouble.' So there goes trouble. May he never come back."

"So that was Morten Bruus," said Anna. "He did not look half as ugly as the stories I've heard tell of him."

"Neither is the devil," said Vibeke, "so black as he's painted. But he's the devil all the same."

On Whitsunday of the year 1625, Parson Sören Qvist baptized the child of Hans and Ida Möller with water and salt into the community of Christ. Majestic in the authority which he assumed on Sundays, robed in the long black ornat with the white gauffered collar which Anna kept fresh and crisp for him with much patient care, he took the heavily swaddled little infant into the hands which had helped deliver the Star, daughter of Golden Rose, which had handled the plow and the udders of his kine, which was stained with earth as well as with the herbs of his garden, and he administered the sacramental salt with great tenderness. The infant cried at the bitter taste. He instructed the mother and the godparents in their duties, and he touched upon the matter of the exorcism of infants before baptism, and thanked God that they were all good Danes living under a humane and enlightened monarch. Then Ida Möller sat down and gave her child the breast to keep it quiet while the parson concluded the service.

94

Chapter Seven

The sun was bright upon the Vejlby congregation as they emerged, blinking, from the church, and bright upon the rugged limestone walls; unequivocal and bright upon the holiday garments, the sudden reds and cloudlike whites, the strong greens and browns and russets, and bright upon the new green of the grass and shrubs in the churchyard. Anna had been invited to join the christening party. In the center of the group as she approached stood Hans Möller's wife with bewildered eyes, hugging her baby to her breast, feeling herself half a widow, uncertain yet as to whether she was disgraced in her communion by the so-recent charges brought against her husband, and confused to find herself the target of so many kind speeches, so much festivity. Vibeke and the other servants from the parsonage came also to offer their congratulations, before starting home. Parson Sören smiled also as he passed, but did not stop to speak. He had other business in hand.

About an hour later his white mare stopped in Rosmos before the house of Judge Tryg Thorwaldsen, and the pastor alighted, shook out the folds of his black robe which he had worn tucked up about his hips, and handed the rein of the mare to the judge's groom. The judge himself came down to the door to greet his guest.

"Why did you not tell me you were coming today?" he said. "We might have ridden together. I was at Vejlby to hear you preach, but I did not stay for the christening."

"I saw you," replied the pastor, "and it put me in

mind that I have something to talk over with you. And no time like the present. Let us go up, shall we?"

The judge followed his friend up the steep and narrow stairway to the long, oak-paneled room which overlooked the street.

"Stay and dine with me," said the judge.

"Kindly suggested," said the pastor, "but I have this matter so on my mind that I would rather speak first and think of eating afterward."

"Have at least a glass of wine with me," said Thorwaldsen, "for after such discoursing you must be thirsty."

"True enough," admitted the pastor with a smile. "The communion wine refreshes the soul but leaves the body requiring more liquid—either wine or beer."

He seated himself in the high-backed chair at one end of the long oak table. Tryg took the chair at the opposite end, and together they waited while Tryg's housekeeper brought them glasses and a decanter of yellow Spanish wine. Tryg was a tall young man, bony and fair-haired, with clear blue eyes with a steady focus that bespoke good health and absolute honesty of heart. He was young to be a judge, but twenty-six years old. Because of his father's early death he was in full control of a moderate fortune and estate, and was well respected in the county.

The parson poured himself a glass of wine and shoved the decanter down the table. "You were at Randers, were you not, when the case of Hans Möller came up for settlement?" Tryg nodded, and the parson continued, "You know that they sent him to the

King's shipyard for ten years. The work there being
what it is, God knows if he will ever come back to see
that child of his I christened today." The parson
frowned, and sighed, and took a sip of the wine. "Hans
told me, before the trial, that Morten Bruus of Ingvorstrup lent him that sum of money. It seems to me
he was downright foolish to accept money from Bruus,
of all people, without a paper of some sort. Unless,
indeed, Bruus cleverly talked him into it."

"I've done some wondering about this," said Tryg.
"You say there was no paper?"

"So Möller told me, and I took him to task about it."

"But now," said Tryg, "Bruus himself comes forward with a paper. No longer ago than yesterday he
brought me a document with Möller's mark on it, and
that of his wife as well. It was a mortgage for twice the
sum that Bruus had said he lent him."

The parson lifted his brows. "A mortgage, so? But
there was no talk of a mortgage. Simply that the
money, in silver pieces, had been left on the table, that
Morten's servants testified to the presence of Möller
about the place on that day, and that later Möller was
known to be paying off certain small debts in the
village, and that he had money in the house, which,
added to the sums paid in the village, made out the
full sum that had been lying on the table in Morten's
house. All circumstantial evidence it was, with the
word of Hans against Morten, and the King's man
knowing little of Morten's reputation—if anything at
all."

"Morten's last story," Tryg replied, "is this. Three

97

years ago come St. John's he lent the money to Hans, taking a mortgage on his land, the strip nearest to the house. Then comes a strip belonging to Ingvorstrup, then one that came to Hans through his wife. Now Morten means to ask for Ida's piece of land as payment for the stolen money. When he has Möller's piece, he'll have a clear field, all three together. The mortgage on Möller's does not fall due for another four years, but there is a part payment due on it this year. When I asked him why this was not brought forward at the trial, he said that it had nothing to do with the theft, legally. He implies that Hans stole the money in order to pay back the mortgage."

"Hans never mentioned such a mortgage to me," said the pastor. "And now he is not here to be questioned."

"Exactly," said Tryg. "And furthermore, Ida Möller denies her mark."

"Her word against that of Morten," said the pastor, "and Hans already discredited in the eyes of the law."

"What does Morten say to that?"

"He says that it is natural, since Hans denies the theft."

"And what do you say to it? Did you see the mortgage?"

"I would say," replied Tryg, "that the paper has a wonderfully new look for any paper which had been in the possession of Morten Bruus for the last three years."

The parson smiled. "Come now," he said. "Morten would take better care of a mortgage than of himself.

Yet it looks very strange. Tryg, my good friend, this goes on now for the last six or seven years, ever since Morten is master of Ingvorstrup, although this is by far the most serious. In little things Morten is forever getting the better of my peasants. I can never put my finger on the exact ill deed. He thinks himself quite safe, too."

"He is a clever varmint," said Tryg.

"He thinks himself so safe," resumed the pastor, "that he comes to me, to me, mind you, and asks—if you can believe it—asks for my Anna in marriage."

The effect upon the judge was as the pastor had wished it. His eyes almost started out of his head. He opened his mouth to exclaim, but the pastor lifted a hand. "Furthermore, he does it in such a way that I lose all my good sense in anger and heave him out the door upon his head. I thought he did it to taunt me, the shifty fox. Now I think he was in earnest. But he brought me closer to man-killing than I have come in many a year, and I find it hard to forgive him for that, as hard as to forgive him for having such thoughts about my girl. I was a great fool." Again the hand lifted to silence his listener. "I was a fool indeed, for I have made him a bitterer enemy, and not for myself alone, but for my people. He came talking soft words about Möller. He offered to withdraw the charges, knowing full well, I am sure, that that could not be done. But now he comes out with an unheard-of mortgage. Do you see how that looks?"

"As if he had thought up the mortgage yestereve, or the night before," said Tryg. "Still, I would break his neck myself, if I could, for daring to think so of Anna."

The parson smiled a singularly sweet and happy smile for a man who had been so incensed.

"Would you indeed, my dear Tryg? I wish I might give you leave."

"By my life, I would," said Tryg.

"Yet you would not dance with her on May Eve."

"Dancing about the fires is for the folk," said Tryg Thorwaldsen. "Damn it all, Parson Sören, I'm a magistrate."

"Yet you will have to dance at your own wedding," said the parson benevolently.

Tryg stared at the old man, rising from his seat, both hands flat on the table, while the inference struck home. A great shyness entered his face and voice.

"Would you consider . . ." he began with deference. "Might I . . . Oh, the devil take it. Would you consider, Parson Sören, betrothing her to me?"

"Am I not asking it?" said the parson. "Morten's offer gave me a jar. I had been so happy with her myself I had clean forgot that I should have been looking after her future happiness. It seems such a little while that she was a small maid. And here she is turned seventeen. Almost too old to marry."

The linden crowns grew thick about the steep roofs of the parsonage, and in the corners of walls and by the edge of the pond the burdock grew tall. The geese took shelter under the coarse rough leaves, and the children made baskets of the green burrs. Cinquefoil, with small yellow blossom, and ranunculus, with glossy yellow cup, edged the sunny roads, and the weather was warm so that the cattle remained in the fields all night. It was early June when the betrothal of Judge Tryg Thorwaldsen and Anna Sörensdaughter was celebrated. At Tryg's wish, the betrothal dinner was given at his house in Rosmos, and the papers were signed in the narrow, high-paneled room with the three glazed windows. But Sören Qvist kept open house at the parsonage that evening.

Folk were there from as far away as Hallendrup, Tryg's friends from Rosmos, and Pastor Sören's great friend Peder Korf, from the parsonage at Aalsö, a short, sturdy man with a thick brown beard and bright blue eyes. Vibeke was attentive to all. She seemed to be everywhere at once, and indefatigable. She brought hot buttered cabbage to Pastor Korf, and twisted cakes and tankards of beer to the gentry from Rosmos. She stepped into the garden to cut fresh cabbage for the pot which she kept boiling all the evening, and surprised Kirsten and Hans kissing, as they thought, unobserved. She only laughed at Kirsten for blushing so that even the back of her neck was red, and hurried on her way. She carried drink to the musicians, and routed Anna from the dairy, where the girl had taken refuge in a familiar task from so much festivity.

"This is the place for Kirsten tonight," said Vibeke, "not for you. And you should be where Kirsten is, courting in the garden."

"Oh, Vibeke," said the girl, "I have been kissed by a hundred people since noon, if I've been kissed by one. I wanted a moment to think things over a little."

"A button for thinking," said Vibeke. "Go and dance with your man."

A trestle table had been set up in the courtyard, and spread with a white linen cloth that fairly touched the ground. Here were baskets of Vibeke's cakes, and all the tankards that the parsonage could boast or borrow, silver and beechwood, silver and ebony, patterned earthenware with silver lids, and here also the guests, as they arrived, brought offerings of fruit, the first strawberries, and, on beds of green leaves, the first cherries. Here were the bowls of hot cabbage drowned in butter, and rounds of creamy cheese, and platters of smoked fish and of salt fish, where all who came might help themselves. On the farther side of the yard, near the big heap of manure, with the wall of the byre behind them, sat the musicians, two fiddlers and the man with the tuba who also played in the church on Sundays. A bagpiper from Grenaa had come as well. They were contributing the music as a betrothal gift. It was not every day that Parson Sören had a daughter to affiance, and there were few in Vejlby parish, or in Aalsö parish, for that matter, who had not known Anna since she was a little girl.

Judge Thorwaldsen danced. He danced the "Little Man in a Fix" with Kirsten, Vibeke, and Hans. Then he danced the "Crested Hen" with Anna and Vibeke, and he danced round dances until his linen was soaked with sweat and the edges of his fair hair as well. He would fain have rested, but Vibeke had an eye upon him. He marveled that Vibeke did not drop in her tracks. She seemed to be in every dance. Well into her forties, and not so slender as she once had been by a good many pounds, she was still as quick on her feet as any young woman in the crowd, and although her round face grew pink and her forehead dewy, her breath came as evenly as a girl's. The music, backed by the wall of the byre, re-echoing from the other three walls, was bravely loud, and the musicians were as unflagging as Vibeke.

The merrymaking began toward the end of the afternoon, and went on, to the accompaniment of the evening chores, into the long, gilded twilight. At ten in the evening the sun still touched the tops of the lindens.

103

Tryg had lost Anna among the dancers. He found her again after some search, standing with her father in the company of three ragged men. The beggars had heard the sound of the music a long way off, and had come, hoping for refreshment. Pastor Sören, mindful of the wedding guests once sought out by the hedges and byways, called for Anna to fetch them drink. He stood conversing with them while Anna went to fulfill his request, a taller man than any of them, in his long black gown and white ruff, his white head overlooking them all, and one of the dusty wayfarers said, "You must be none other than Parson Sören Qvist. I made a friend in Grenaa, who told me that I might get shelter with you for a night. But I did not know that this was the farm or that we were to find a feast."

"And who was your friend?" said Sören.

"A true beggar, a fellow with twisted legs that can hardly walk. He said that you had taken him in more times than he could remember. But, Parson, we are not beggars by profession. Just men for the present without any funds."

One of his companions laughed. "A good way to describe a beggar," he said. "But no, we are not beggars by intention. We are on our way south to join the King."

Landless men, and without families, they had come from north of Aalborg in response to Christian's call for volunteers, and they hoped, with luck, to overtake his army in Holstein within the month. The pastor looked sober at the mention of the King's campaign.

"It seemed to me," he said, "a war we did not need.

Chapter Eight

The Council too was against it, so I hear. And the burden on the country is very great. It comes too soon after the Kalmar war, as well. The taxes fall, as ever, heaviest on the peasant, though the house of God has not escaped a levy. They took the bells from my church, all save one, to melt down into cannon, and that, my friends, seems to me the wrong conversion for metal that was used to call the people to prayer."

"Is it not a war for the faith?" said one of the strangers, and "Down with the Papists!" said another. "Assuredly it is a war against the Emperor and the League."

"I wonder sometimes if it is not mainly a war to keep the Swedes from feeling themselves too big," said the pastor. "Now here is my daughter Anna with the best brew in the county of Randers."

"Health to the lady," said the man who had spoken first, "and happiness as well."

"Health to this man also," said the pastor, as he saw Tryg approaching them. He introduced him to the strangers, and then, clapping the young magistrate heavily upon the shoulder, "Did I not say you would dance, Tryg?"

"I have danced myself weak," said Tryg. "I would like a word with Anna, if I may take her from you," and so led her away, although she protested.

"Now it begins," said the parson. "You see how he takes her from me? Well, I cannot keep her forever." After a pause he went on, "I shall be shorthanded in more quarters than one before the year is over. One of my men joined up last April, when the first talk of war came our way. I have only Hans among the men. I could use another farm servant, if one of you would be willing to stay."

"Thank you kindly, Parson," said the stranger. "For myself, I have an itching foot. Having set my mind upon seeing the Weser, I'd rather go on. I'm still too near to Aalborg to feel that I have traveled far enough."

His companions laughed, and agreed with him. They thanked the parson, but they had had enough of hay-rakes and spades to last them out the year.

Sören did not urge them. He led them up to the table and bade them help themselves. He told them also that they might share the servants' quarters with Hans, and that they might turn in whenever they were tired. "As for Vibeke," he concluded, "like enough she will dance until sunup, if she can persuade Lars Pedersen and the rest to play that long."

He left his chance guests regaling themselves on salt fish and cabbage, and, feeling a little tired himself, as well as a little sad, he began to look for a bench where he might sit down. The couples were forming in squares for a new dance, and Anna and Tryg had not returned. He traversed the court, wishing to get a fair distance from the musicians. Under one of the lindens, at the edge of the road, was a seat built around the trunk of the tree from which he thought he might watch his guests in some coolness and seclusion. Before he reached this refuge, however, he was accosted by a young peasant, who removed his large hat of greenish felt and stood with head bowed, as if he meant to ask a favor or a blessing.

"What is it, my man?" said the parson. "Have they not made you welcome at the table?"

"Welcome enough," said the man, "and thanks for the food. But if it like Your Worship, I should wish to be taken into Parson's service."

"How so?" said Sören Qvist, feeling some surprise because he had just had his offer of employment refused.

"Should like to work for Parson, that is all," said the man.

He lifted his head, and even in the dimming light the parson recognized a likeness, of a sort, to a face which he knew.

"Are you not the brother of Morten Bruus?" he asked.

"That is right, Parson," answered the man.

"And you wish to work for me?"

"That is right too, Parson."

"And what would your brother say to that?"

"Morten cares nothing at all for what I do," said Niels. "He will not have me about. He gives me nothing. He does nothing for me. He's an unnatural brother."

Sören Qvist regarded him thoughtfully for a moment. Then he inquired, "Do you like to work, Niels?"

"That I do not, Pastor," said Niels, honestly enough. "But I like to eat."

Sören smiled a little at that. Niels looked enough like Morten to have aroused his instant dislike. But he was also shabby, unlike Morten, and the poor, whether deserving or not, all had a free way to the parson's sympathy.

"Why do you come to me," he asked, "rather than to another?"

Niels looked down at his hat, twisting and turning it before he answered. "Parson is known as a good master," he said at last.

Sören hesitated yet. It seemed to him an odd thing that the brother of his enemy wished to become a part of his household. But it was true that he needed an extra man about the farm. The season was growing apace. It would soon be time for the haying. There was always more to be done than he and Hans could manage, and it left him with ever less time for the needs of his parishioners. Then he thought that perhaps providence had sent the man his way in order that he might make some small atonement for his anger. Vicariously, he might forgive his enemy without giving quarter to the evil for which his enemy stood.

"Very well," he said kindly. "You may work for me, Niels. And as long as the work is honest, all else will be too. You'll receive the same wages as the others, and good food, and a good roof. You may tell Hans to give you a bed tonight."

Niels bent his head and made a sort of bow. Then he betook himself to the servants' quarters to look for Hans.

The moon was in its last quarter that night and did not rise as the sun went down, but the stars began to come out, white in the softening blue of the sky. As the blue deepened to violet, and the violet grew wan, but luminous and translucent, more stars appeared in clusters and in drifts and sparkled like frost. A mist rose from the pond, and the dew gathered on leaves and grass. Anna and Tryg went down the road toward the parson's garden, Anna compelled by Tryg's hand in the crook of her elbow. She held her hands clasped before her waist and looked down, as she went, at the two gold betrothal bracelets shining on her wrists. Tryg, following her glance, said, "Do you like them?" and she answered, without lifting her head, "Yes, they are very pretty."

The road before them ran on into dimness. The hill rose gently under a grassy slope to the dark shadow of the wood, and all about them, in the warm night, was the sense of the bounty of the land. When they came opposite the stile in the hedge, Anna detached herself from Tryg's grasp and mounted the high steps. The wood was very wet; she brushed it dry with her hand as best she could before she sat down. Tryg came and stood beside her, resting his hand on the broad step, the thick hazel leaves crowding behind him. Anna folded her hands in her lap. She was aware of the hand beside her, and that she might very easily have laid her own upon it, and the reasons for her not doing so were various and obscure, even to herself. She waited for Tryg to speak, but he did not seem to know where to begin. In the quiet, she could almost hear him rejecting first one opening and then another. Finally he said, quite simply, "You avoid me. When I see you dancing, I think that you look very happy.

But when I try to come near you, you slip away from me. I have to ask you, are you sorry about this betrothal?"

"You know quite well," she answered quietly, "that my father would never have betrothed me without my consent."

"Well, then, consenting, why do you run away?"

"I knew," she said, "that his heart was set upon it. And we have been good friends."

"We have known each other a long time," he replied gravely, "and we have been friends, and good friendships make the best marriages." As she looked down at her hands again and did not reply, he said, "Is that not true?"

"I had always thought so," she answered slowly.

His face, though indistinct, was near to her, and it appeared very troubled. "But something has happened to make you change your mind?" he inquired, still more gravely.

"Yes, perhaps," she said, and she was suddenly, to her own surprise, filled with a sense of alarm that was yet sweet and made her tremble although she was not cold. Tryg's eyes upon her, searching her face through the growing darkness, increased her agitation, and because of it she closed her own eyes and turned her head away. Tryg did not stir, nor speak for some time, and when he did his voice was flat and cold, and unfamiliar.

"It is fortunate," he said, "that a betrothal is only a piece of paper, and we can burn it. And so we will." He lifted his hand from the stile and moved a step or two away from her. He repeated, without emphasis, "And so we will. Well, good night, Anna." ·

"You do not understand," she said, turning toward him again.

"I try to," he said, from the depths of his hurt. "I think I do." And he added, "I do not blame you. You are very young."

"But, Tryg," she exclaimed, distressed and a little frightened, "I am sure that you do not understand."

"You are not in love with me," he said. "Or you are in love with someone else."

"But how can I know?" she cried, springing to her feet. The movement made her much taller than he. She looked down into a face that she could hardly decipher.

"But I know that I am in love with you," he said.

"But, Tryg," she cried again, and then stopped. "Hans kisses Kirsten in the garden, or the dairy," she said. "You have never kissed me, save this noon, before twenty people."

"It would hardly have been proper," he said.

"You have never before even said that you loved me. Oh," she exclaimed in swift exasperation, and stamped her foot, "I would rather be Kirsten!"

Then Tryg put his hands about her waist and lifted her clear of the stile, and holding her to him, her feet still clear of the ground, kissed her as she wished, upon the mouth. He had never touched her before; he had never realized how small and light she was. He set her on her feet at last, and took her face in his hands.

"It is strange," he said. "Your face looks very cool

and white, like those early anemones in the beech-wood, but your lips are warm."

On the far side of the house the violins began the measures for the "Crested Hen," and after a few bars the pipes joined in. No one came to interrupt the lovers.

Anna did not know when the dancing stopped and the last guests departed. She woke once and noticed that everything was still, but the pallor which showed through the crack between the shutters was not that of morning. Then she slept again, and woke late. There were voices in the kitchen. She heard the chain clink as someone ran a bucket down the well, and she heard the jingling of harness as a team was led out to the fields.

She lay still for a few minutes longer, stretching herself under the light warm covering of the feather quilt. Then she reached up and unfastened her nightcap, dropped it on the floor beside her, and spread out her hair on the pillow, running her fingers through it to loosen the coils. The room was dim. The sun never reached this corner of the house until late afternoon, but there was already an indication that the day would be warm. She stirred a little and the folds of linen fell about her body softly like waves of lukewarm water. Remembrance of the day before returned to her, of her

113

surprise to find it so simple and natural a thing to be kissing Tryg many times. She remembered the smell of his face, healthy and warm, and how large and secure his shoulder had seemed as she hung upon it. If anyone had asked her the day before yesterday what she had expected it would be like to be betrothed, she would not have known what to answer, except, perhaps, that she expected it to be different from anything she had hitherto known. But this morning it all seemed familiar, very safe, very pleasant, and altogether natural. She yawned, and pushed back the down quilt, and, drowsily, got out of bed.

White as a withe of peeled willow, small and very slender, touched with gold, naked in the half-light, she moved across the brick floor, swaying slightly as if she were still half asleep. It was certainly going to be a warm day, for she felt no inclination to put on her clothes in a hurry. She picked up a white linen smock and slipped it over her head, drawing the long golden-red hair out of the gathered neck and spreading it loose on her shoulders. She shook out a linen petticoat and stepped into it, tying it tight about her waist. Then followed two colored skirts of camlet, one yellow and one green; then a russet bodice, fastening tight about the waist. The pressure of her hands on her waist as she adjusted the bodice reminded her of the hands of Tryg, last night, and she smiled, her head on one side, and stood a moment, dreaming.

She pushed back the wooden shutters and stood beside the window as she combed and braided her hair, looking out across the morning meadows. The voices in the kitchen were many, and unfamiliar. She thought that they were probably those of the ragged strangers to whom she had served the drinks the evening before. The parson kept so many guests—beggars or travelers —that, at certain seasons of the year when work on the farms was slack, the servants' room was as frequented as an inn. She bound the braids about her head, but did not put on a cap, and went barefoot into the kitchen for a cup of milk.

There were four strangers in the kitchen, three of whom she remembered from the night before; the fourth was the young man whom she had seen with Morten Bruus in front of the inn. Vibeke and Kirsten had given them beer and bread and salt fish, and were sitting gossiping. Very little work had been done, apparently. Vibeke rose and fetched her young mistress bread and cheese, saying over her shoulder as she went to the food chest, "Here is Niels Bruus who is going to work for us."

One of the strangers said, "Aye, mistress, we have been trying to persuade him to go along with us to the wars, but he will not, the poltroon."

"I will stay and work for Parson," said Niels, as he had already affirmed half a dozen times that morning. "I will be an honest man and do an honest man's work. You can go and steal from corpses."

"Have a care now," said the stranger. "We are going to defend the Christian faith, and we are already soldiers by spirit, even if we are not yet enlisted. We will call you out for such another crack, and crack your head."

"Best think it over, Niels," said Vibeke. "If you stay with Parson you will surely have to do an honest man's work. And that's more than I ever heard of your doing before."

"Well," said Niels doggedly, "I have thought it over and I am going to work."

"Hear, hear!" said Vibeke. "But remember, the parson is short with those who are loafers—except on mornings after betrothals."

"I have heard he has a quick hand," said Niels. "Still, I will stay."

He rolled his eyes at Kirsten then in such a manner that she gave him a push that nearly knocked him off his stool, and then she left the room.

"You can soon be at your work, then," said Vibeke. "There is no more to eat here until noon."

"And at noon?" said Niels.

"Kirsten will bring you your lunch in the field."

"Aye, yes, the field. Now what did Parson say I must do in the field?"

"You heard as well as I," said Vibeke. "Be on your way."

"All in good time," said Niels, getting up slowly. "Well, be sure it is Kirsten." He went slowly out the door.

The strangers, too, then bethought themselves of leaving. They made proper thanks to Vibeke, and formal compliments and good wishes to Anna, and went off.

Vibeke looked after them a trifle wistfully. Anna

said, to tease her, "How is it, Vibeke? Do you wish to go to the wars also?"

Vibeke, turning from the door, smiled tenderly at Anna and, coming closer, put her arm around the girl's shoulders and kissed her on the cheek. "You are a good lass," she said, "although not at all like your mother. They are going to Aebeltoft. It is a good twenty miles, maybe twenty-five from here, but they will be there tonight. I was thinking that I should like to see the old town again. I have not seen it since the day your mother was married."

"I should like to see it too," said Anna. "I should like to see all the towns of Jutland. I used to think that I would marry a man from far away, and get to see the world. And here I am, all promised to Tryg, and I shan't move any farther from home than the five miles to Rosmos."

"You should be happy to be promised to Tryg," said Vibeke.

"Oh, I am. But all the same, I am a little sad to think that everything is settled, and I know for certain what the rest of my life will be like." She laughed, and added, "Whatever possessed my father to hire Niels Bruus? How long is he to stay?"

"He's to stay as long as he works," said Vibeke. "And don't ask me what possessed the parson. He might have been out of his mind. Unless," she suggested thoughtfully, "he was that sorry that he threw Morten out on his head. That would be like your father. Well, his mind doesn't work like yours and mine. Will you have more milk?"

117

Later in the day, as Anna and Vibeke sat in the Bride's Room, the memory of Aebeltoft still engaged the housekeeper. They had opened the chest which had held the dowry of Anna's mother, and had gone to the very bottom of it, spreading out the sheets and table covers, the embroidered pillow slips and hand towels upon the bed and upon the other chest, counting every item carefully, and debating upon how much new would be needed to supplement the inherited linens and make a supply worthy of Tryg's house. There were things other than household linens in the chest. There were ruffles and ruffs such as had been worn, twenty-seven years ago, with gowns cut low in front. There were infant's clothes and swaddling bands, and a round ruffled bonnet which Vibeke perched upon her hand and smiled at, as if she saw the face beneath.

"Are you looking at the past or the future?" said Anna, seated on the floor in a square of sunshine.

"At the past," said Vibeke. "First Peder's, then yours. Both fair, round, rosy faces. Both round, fat, healthy children. But Peder stayed solid, and you, since you were going on five years, grow slimmer all the time. Well, I will like to see you wedded, and wax round."

Anna laughed. "Was Peder really so much more like my mother?" she coaxed.

"As like as a man could be to a woman, and still be a man." She sighed and looked at her fist sadly. "Well, it was one thing to be a woman and wedded to your father. She was quiet in a way that was good for him, and, being a woman, she could bear with more."

"You speak," said Anna, "as if it were a great trial to live with my father."

"No," said the housekeeper. "When all's said and done, he is the best man, for goodness, for kindness, for openhandedness, that I have ever known. But you know yourself that it is either a sunny day or a storm with him." Seeing Anna unconvinced, she added, "He is less stormy now than when your brother was a lad. Yes, he grows gentler with age, but he is not entirely an old man yet!"

"Is it true, then, that Peder left home because of my father's anger?"

"Is that what they tell you in the village?" said Vibeke. "Yes, and no. It is partly true. Your father was never angered at Peder, but Peder did not like the stormy days. Those your mother could manage. She had a great calmness in her spirit. But Peder was a man, and he could not withdraw into himself like that. So he packed up, when he was as old as you are now, and walked down the road one morning, and that was the end of it. That is the way I think it happened. My life upon it, your father was never angry with your brother. He loved him too well."

"I can't remember him very clearly," said Anna, frowning a little.

"You were not over five, yourself," said Vibeke. "It is no wonder."

"Do you know where he went?"

"I think it was to Sweden. There was some talk that he might have enlisted and gone with the King to Kalmar. He may have been killed, God rest us all, or

119

he may have stayed in Skaane. We shall never know. I think he must have been killed, since he has never come home nor sent a letter. Your mother died thinking that he must have been killed."

"Tell me about my mother," said Anna, drawing up her knees and resting her chin on them. "Tell me about Aebeltoft and the wedding."

The housekeeper laid the bonnet down, gently and sadly. "It was a wedding such as I hope you will have," she said. "I was but newly in your mother's service, and it would have seemed to me the gayest day in all my life whether there had been any merrymaking or not. Such a lady she was. I have never known another like her." She pulled up the two outer skirts that draped her knees and reached for the hem of her linen petticoat. With it she wiped her eyes. "Look how you make me cry," she said. "You and your questions."

"Then tell me about Aebeltoft before you knew my mother," said Anna.

But Vibeke shook her head. "Some other day, perhaps. But not now."

"That is what you always tell me—some other day. Come, tell me about Aebeltoft. It is twenty times finer than Grenaa, I am sure."

"All this," said Vibeke, looking about the room, and disregarding Anna, "should be washed and sunned. It is growing yellow. Then you will have to be quicker with your wheel this summer. We have some wool— we can take it to Grenaa and have it dyed red, or blue. But when will you be married?"

"I don't know," said Anna. "I can't decide. Martinmas, perhaps. I have a notion to make Tryg court me for a few months. He'll come by me too easily if I marry this summer."

"You are not a sensible person," said Vibeke, and the meaning of her words was belied by the affection in her voice. "You are a fly in the wind. You haven't a thought weightier than a piece of thistledown. The strange thing is, I sometimes see your mother in your face, but I never hear her in your voice. Now you may keep the keys to the chest. And don't lose them."

Still later, that same day, they were all in the parsonage kitchen, Anna, Vibeke, Hans, and Kirsten, waiting for the parson and Niels to come before Vibeke should ladle up the soup. The door to the courtyard was open, as usual; the chickens walked mincingly across the doorstep, and the brown dog lay with his head on Anna's feet as she sat in the alcove behind the fireplace. Drowsy and dreamy from being up late the night before, and from this new sense of being in love, she sat with her chin on her hand and her elbow on her knee, enjoying the weight of the warm furred head against her foot. She watched Kirsten come and go about the table, now in the sunlight from the opened door, now in the shadow, and now, bending to help Vibeke, with the light of the fire on her fair hair, making it, for a moment, almost as red a gold as her own. Hans sat beyond the table on a stool, his hands hanging loosely before him. He was tired. He too had danced late and had done a long day's work in the sun. None of them wanted to talk, not even Vibeke, but there was a drowsy content common to

them all. When Vibeke took the lid from the kettle
the smell of cabbage steamed into the air already heavy
with wood smoke and the tang of salt herring.

As they waited thus, the parson appeared suddenly
in the doorway. Anna rose to greet him, as she did so
disturbing the dog, who stretched himself and began
a yawn. Before the beast could finish stretching, however, the parson, with a face like a thundercloud,
crossed the room, entered the corridor, passed down it
with long strides, entered his study, and shut the door
with a sound like the clap of thunder. It was like the
passage of a violent wind. No one would have been
more surprised if the cups and bowls had risen from
the table and eddied in the air like dry leaves.

"Whatever——" began Anna, looking to Vibeke.

"Did I not tell you?" said Vibeke. "It is either a
sunny day——"

"Almighty God," said Hans, "he has not been that
way in half a year."

Anna sighed, and Vibeke said, "If I know anything,
we will not see him again this night. Shall I serve now?"

"Do," said Hans, "for God's mercy. My belly thinks
my throat's slit."

"There is no need to wait for Niels," said Anna. She
carried two bowls to Vibeke, who ladled soup into
them. Kirsten poured milk for herself and Anna, beer
for Hans. They drew about the table in their accustomed places and began to eat.

After a time Kirsten said, "I hope he does not think
it my fault."

"Think what thy fault?" said Vibeke.

"That Niels was talking to me."

"And when?" said Vibeke.

"In the dairy, a half hour gone, or more. I hope he does not think that I have tried to make Niels follow me about."

Vibeke laid down her spoon beside her bowl. "Come, now," she said, "and tell us about it. Where is Niels now, that he does not follow you to supper?"

"I took him his lunch, as you told me," said Kirsten, "to the field where Parson sent him. He wasn't working then, but resting under the oak tree. I don't think he had done a great deal of work."

Hans snorted and choked on his soup. "I passed the field on my way home," he said. "He must have spent more time scratching himself than working at the earth."

"But I did not stay to talk with him while he ate, not very long," Kirsten resumed. "He said he would follow me home, but I sent him back. Then, when I went to milk, he came to the pasture and watched me, and he offered to carry the pails for me."

"So you let him?" Vibeke prompted her.

"Well, yes. The pails were very full. But I told him not to stay."

"Yet he stayed?" said Vibeke.

"So he did, and Parson caught him there."

"Well," said Vibeke, "now it comes."

"Parson gave him a buffet of one ear that spun him round. Then he caught him by the other ear and spun him the other way. Then he took him by both shoulders and pushed him out the door."

"Yet Parson said nothing to you or to him?"

"Oh, he said plenty to Niels, nothing to me. And indeed, Niels was very disrespectful to Parson. Then Parson went off in the direction of the pasture. I didn't look to see what Niels did. I tell you, I was so frightened I couldn't hit the line for the cream, my hand shook so, in the skimming."

Hans said, "You're a sly one, knowing all this, and keeping as mum as a mouse."

"I hoped Parson might walk it off," said Kirsten, "as he sometimes does, you know. It was all so quiet and pleasant in here." She looked appealingly at Vibeke. "Why should I talk about it, unless Parson meant to?"

Vibeke nodded, then sighed. "He is angry with himself, more than with Niels, I think, and that is not so easy to walk off." She caught a skeptical glance from Hans and continued, "You wonder how I know? Have I not worked for him for seven and twenty years? I think I should know."

"Well," said Hans, "I cannot say I am sorry. I did not much care for Niels as a bunk mate."

"As far as concerns Niels, I am not sorry either," said the housekeeper. "Sooner or later, it would have come. Why not the sooner?"

Anna said nothing at all at supper. She helped Kirsten and Vibeke to clear away after the meal, and she spun at the small wheel until the light in the alcove grew too dim to see by. Before she went to bed, she tapped at her father's door. He made no answer, and she went sadly to sleep. Like the others, she was relieved that Niels was not to stay, but her relief was shadowed by her father's mood which seemed to reach, like a cloud, into every corner of the parsonage.

"We were all too happy last night," she thought before she fell asleep.

The next day the parson, being in Grenaa, hired a new servant by the name of Lars Sondergaard. He was a short man, with a head as hard and round as a nut, and a body to match. He worked well, he was clean and cheerful, and Hans welcomed him to the servants' quarters.

In less than a week Niels returned to the parsonage. He came to the field where Hans and the pastor were cultivating. Hans saw him advance through the young rye and approach the parson with his hat in his hand and his head bent. He expected to see him depart again promptly, but the parson spoke to him at length, and, it seemed, very kindly.

"Parson Sören," said Niels, his eyes on his old black felt hat, "my brother Morten will have nothing to do with me. Since I came to you, he says I'm no brother of his. He wouldn't give me a crust of bread or a drink of cold water, not if my mouth was hanging open in hell. Go back to Parson, he says, and be damned to you. So here I am. Kindly," said Niels, never shifting his eyes from the hat which he twisted and turned in his hands, "kindly take me back, Parson. I did very wrong to slight my work. I promise to do better."

Sören Qvist looked down at the bent head, the lank black hair falling on the unclean collar, the shoulders stooped in humility, and felt a deep dislike for this brother of Morten Bruus. It seemed to him an obscurely deep and unreasonable dislike. Yet since Niels had been cast off by his brother because of having had employment with the parson, Sören Qvist felt that he was to some extent responsible for the man. Niels was repentant. His humility seemed genuine. Here was the parson's opportunity to make a good servant of him. In the privacy of his study Sören had protested upon his knees that he repented heartily of his anger toward this man. "For how little a thing," he had cried in the distress of his spirit, "did I strike and dismiss him! Surely I made him suffer for being the brother of Morten Bruus, which was no fault of his. Had it been Hans, or Lars, who had slighted his duty to flirt a little with Kirsten, would I have been moved to such bitter anger?" Now, at the return of Niels, he told himself, "I am given the occasion to make my repentance true in deed as in prayer. I should rejoice." Yet it was with sorrow that he replied, actually, to his servant:

"Well enough, Niels. I take you back into my household. But remember, I expect as good service from you as from the others."

Niels lifted his head then to thank the parson, and the old man, looking down at him, tried to read in his face the reason for the deep dislike he had aroused together with the reason for the strange compulsion he felt to reinstate him. The face lifted to his was stupid, he thought, rather than malicious. The eyes were a dull green, like the tarnish on base metals, the skin darkened by exposure to the sun, rather than warmed or brightened. In one ear he wore a leaden earring,

127

and the whole face seemed, to the intent gaze of the parson, heavy and dark as that metal. In the purity and lightness of the summer morning, in the field of young grain that rippled sleek and luminous under the morning breeze, Niels stood like a spot in the atmosphere from which all light had been withdrawn. Moved by a great desire to bring some spark of understanding into the dull eyes which at last met his, the parson began to speak of good and bad servants, of how we are all servants before the Lord, and of the servant who came at the eleventh hour and yet was received with the same kindness and given the same reward as those who had labored all the day. Niels listened unwillingly, and later said to Kirsten: "He gave me such a preachment as was wasted without a full congregation. I almost felt the walls of the church closing round me as he talked."

The other servants accepted the return of Niels without much protest. He was good-natured with them, and for a week or so did his fair share of the work. Hans, however, complained to Vibeke that Niels had filled the servants' quarters full of fleas. Without mentioning the matter to the pastor, she and Hans and Lars removed all the straw from the beds, took out the leather sheets to the meadow and brushed them thoroughly, made Niels remove all his clothing and give it to Vibeke to be washed. Lars and Hans meantime scrubbed down their fellow servant in what was probably the first thorough bath of his life. He complained bitterly about the hazards of catching cold, and complained also that his clothes had shrunk and no longer felt comfortable. But as both Niels and the garments began to resume their natural protective patina of earth, soot, and grease, he ceased to complain and began to compliment Vibeke on the food she served. Vibeke also had a kindlier feeling toward him. Sören Qvist went about with an open and sunny countenance, and all seemed well at the parsonage.

In time, however, Niels began again to vex the parson. The trouble began with such little matters that the other servants could not themselves say whether or not Niels was to blame. He was stupid, and easily misunderstood his orders. It was hard to know sometimes whether he misunderstood them intentionally. A reasonable rebuke had little effect upon him. He would stand smiling while the parson explained the extent of damage caused by his misdoing, until Sören, losing patience, would find himself compelled to roar and shake his fist, since nothing but the sound of anger seemed to reach the slow brain. It was plain to all that the parson regretted these rages. Sometimes, in his effort not to lose his temper at Niels, he lost it, for less provocation, at the next servant for far less offense, and Kirsten often went weeping to Vibeke because Parson had scolded her for talking to Niels.

Haying time came, and everyone worked in the fields. The cumulus clouds stood high, their tops snowy, their bases shredded horizontally by the wind that blew from the west, constant reminders that the sunny hours were uncertain and brief; and their shadows passed like those of great slow-winged birds across the meadows. Anna helped carry the jugs and baskets to the men at noon, and Vibeke, with a wide, conical hat perched on top of her blue linen cap, took a hand with the rakes, as did also Kirsten.

On one of these days Anna was collecting the remnants of the noon meal under the big oak tree when she overheard her father and Niels. They were some distance away, so that she did not catch the words, yet near enough so that she could not misunderstand the impudence in the voice of Niels, the suppressed anger in that of her father, and it troubled her deeply. In the last month the parson had grown remote and irascible. The servants had come to avoid him, except as they had to meet him about their usual tasks, and he himself avoided his daughter's company. Yet he had moments of great tenderness and affection for her, as when, pausing beside her where she sat spinning, he said: "I suppose you have considered the day for your wedding. You cannot make it too late to please me."

Still he had grown to be a lonely and brooding figure, and the life at the farm was no longer easy and happy, as it had been.

Another day it happened that Lars Sondergaard and Niels were together in Vejlby market, when Morten Bruus passed by. He stopped to consider his brother.

"I hear," said Morten, "that your master has his rages these days. Well, I wish you joy of him." He smiled curiously and went on, Niels not replying.

Lars returned to the parsonage with the comment that it was becoming known all over two parishes that the parson was a changed man.

Then there came a morning late in the month of August, a golden morning with a tinge of chill in the air, when the grain had been stooked and the parson should have been feeling content that the harvest had been made before the early frosts had touched it. Yet, contrarily, on this morning he found himself so plagued by his servant Niels that he struck him again, as he had not struck him since the day after he had first hired him, and furthermore, in his fury, he promised to beat him until his soul should part from his body. After the first blow and the first exclamation, however, the old man checked himself and, turning away abruptly, left Niels standing beside Hans and returned to the house. Vibeke saw him pass through the kitchen with an expression of the greatest sorrow on his face. He shut himself up in his study and remained there all afternoon. Hans, returning to the house at evening, reported what had happened and added his own comment.

"Niels is a regular devil for the parson. I don't know how he does it, but he is forever making mischief. He is more bother than he's worth. I don't know how many times this summer I've done his work as well as my own, and for no other reason than to keep the parson from raging at him. Let him be gone. We shall have a little peace again."

But Niels had not gone. He had disappeared during the afternoon, reappeared at suppertime. He took his customary place at the table and ate his customary share of the food, although no one spoke to him.

The meal was nearly over when the parson appeared. He seemed surprised to see Niels, but he said nothing at first. Niels got up and, walking around to the spot where the parson stood, bowed his head respectfully. He spoke in a low voice, but everyone present, and that included the entire household of the parsonage, heard him confess his fault, apologize humbly, and ask the parson to retain him as his servant. The parson was long in answering. He looked from the bowed head of Niels to all the faces about the long table, and he must have read in them the hope of a dismissal. However, turning again to the offending servant, he briefly accepted his apology and said that he might remain. Niels thanked him. Then, in the profound unspoken disapproval of his household, the parson slowly went back to his own room.

Niels waited until the last footfall died away and the sound of the closing door isolated them all from the pastor. Revolving then upon one heel, he found Hans standing at his elbow.

"Come," said Hans. "Get yourself out of here. You have kept the old man from his supper, as I think you have often enough kept him from his sleep."

Lars also rose and, putting himself at Niels's other shoulder, suggested that he do as Hans had said. The three of them left the kitchen, Niels in the middle like a man under guard, and the women were left alone.

Anna began to weep. Vibeke in silence went about her work for a time. Then she said, her hand on the girl's shoulder, "I will ladle up a bowl of soup for him. Do you take it to him now, and when you give it to him, ask him from us all to send that good-for-nothing packing."

Anna stood with the bowl of hot liquid held carefully in her two hands in the passageway outside her father's study and called to him for admittance. Contrary to her fear, he opened the door for her, and she entered and set the dish upon his desk.

"Well, lass?" said he, as she stood irresolutely, having received his thanks and wondering how to phrase her errand.

"Vibeke bade me, sir, ask you, for all the other servants and herself, and I do ask you too, to send Niels Bruus away. He serves only to anger you. He is no help about the farm. They would all work better without him."

"I have just given him my word that he might stay," said her father. He put his arm about her shoulders and very gently led her to the door. "I thank Vibeke, and the others, for their good will," he said, "but I have given my word."

His manner was so strangely gentle that she would no more have remonstrated with him than she would have with a sleepwalker. She returned to the kitchen and told Vibeke what the parson had said and sat herself down by the fire.

"I cannot understand," she said, "how the presence of one useless servant can so have changed everything about the farm. A half a year ago there was more content here by this hearth than in the whole parish of Vejlby. Or so it seemed to me."

"Amen," said Vibeke. "Kirsten, get you to bed."

"The sun is yet up," said Kirsten.

"So will it be in the morning before I can stir you." Vibeke parted the curtains before the alcove bed and, leaning into the recess, possessed herself of something which had been fastened above the head of the bed. She partly folded her apron across it as she passed Kirsten and went to sit down in the spinning alcove, near her mistress. Anna wiped her wet cheeks with her fingers and, cupping her chin in her hand, sat silent.

Kirsten looked from the bed to the open doorway. The sunlight had lifted from the courtyard and was passing up the wall of the dairy in a slow tide. She went to the well, ostensibly for a drink, but partly, perhaps, to see if Hans or Lars had issued from the servants' room. But the courtyard was deserted, and when she returned to the kitchen, neither Vibeke nor Anna seemed disposed to break their quiet. Unwillingly, for lack of something to do or someone to speak with, Kirsten took off her clothes and slipped into bed, drawing the serge curtains between her and the kitchen. It was dark then, and the quilts warm. She had been very active all day. She thought it was a pity that Niels should vex the pastor so; he could be fun at times, Niels could, but it was not fun to have the farm in a perpetual turmoil because of him. She fell asleep.

Anna and Vibeke sat on, as the room grew duskier. At last Vibeke said, "Will Judge Thorwaldsen be coming tonight?"

Anna shook her head. "Not tonight. He had business in Randers this week."

Chapter Ten

The silence fell again, until Anna, stirring, said, "What have you there, Vibeke? It looks like a spray of rowan."

"It is a flying rowan," said Vibeke, turning the twig thoughtfully between her fingers. "It was growing in a high crotch of the big oak. I had my eye on it for full five weeks before it was right to pluck it."

"How so?" said Anna.

"It has virtues," said Vibeke, "but only if plucked on Ascension Eve. So I bided my time. It keeps off evil spirits. It is a sure protection against witches' charms. But it is very hard to find. And most folk, that think they know about such things, pick it at the wrong time."

"Then it must make you feel much safer to have it," said Anna tolerantly, remembering her father's gentle attitude toward Vibeke and her fears.

"I had it in my bed," the woman confessed. "But now I want you to take it."

"But why?" said Anna.

"To slip it in Parson's room, in some corner where he won't notice it, lest he laugh at it and throw it out. Oh, I know he thinks there's no good in it. But," she said with lowered voice, "he is not reasonable of late. He is acting like a man bewitched."

Anna protested. "I would rather you kept it—you will feel unguarded without it. And I am not sure it would do him any good. I cannot think—— Hark, what was that?"

"It was only the door to Parson's room," said Vibeke. "It screeches like a hoot owl. It needs oiling.

He is coming this way." And she hid the rowan under her apron, folding her hands on her knees.

Parson Sören came into the kitchen, and as soon as he distinguished the forms of Anna and the house-keeper by the hearth, he drew up a straight chair and sat down beside them. He moved like a man who was very tired, and he had obviously been to bed already. He was wearing a long green dressing gown and a white nightcap pushed back a little from his forehead. He passed a hand over his eyes and dropped it heavily upon his knee.

"I could not sleep," he said.

Anna had never before thought of her father as being old, in spite of his white hair and beard. His eye had always been clear and his cheek ruddy, his whole bear-ing full of vigor. But tonight he seemed very old indeed.

"Tryg is not here?" he asked.

Anna replied, as she had to Vibeke, that Tryg had business to perform at Randers.

The parson nodded. "He told me, but I had forgot. I shall be happy to have you married, my girl, but God only knows what I shall do without you. Well, I have come now, feeling that I should make some explana-tion, to you and to Vibeke, and, as I would wish, to Tryg, also, because I know right well you think my conduct strange. No, do not protest. I grant it must seem strange that I keep in service a wretch whose greatest occupation seems to be to anger me." He paused, and, "It is hard to continue," he said. "First, we must grant that I have an old weakness. Vibeke knows, better than you, my dear, how many times it has caused me grief. It is one of the seven deadly sins. I do not take it lightly, God knows; I have wrestled with it all my life. It comes upon me like an inner storm, suddenly. It blinds and shakes me, and makes me not myself. Oh, it is only by the goodness of God that I have hitherto been spared from committing any great crime in my anger. It has lost me my son—oh, his mother never reproached me for it, but I know right well it was my dreadful angers that drove Peder from this house."

He had spoken in a very low voice, but with great emotion, and when he paused, Anna said pleadingly: "It is for that very reason that we all wish you to send Niels Bruus away. Why should you let yourself be tempted?"

The parson was long in replying, and as she waited, her eyes upon her father's face, Anna thought that it was more than the gleam and shadow from the hearth that made the hollows in the temples seem so deep and the eyes so deeply set. At last the parson said: "It is the will of God. It is the will of God that I shall be tempted until I prove myself able to withstand this evil. Then, perhaps, in my old age I shall have peace, and perhaps even my Peder may be restored to me, that I may see him once again with the eyes of the flesh before I die."

Anna said humbly, "But do we not pray to be delivered from temptation?"

The parson nodded. "I have prayed so too. But I have come to see that God intends me to be tempted now. In little things, when the spirit is open and awake, He shows His plan. If He has sent a devil to tempt me,

137

then, like St. Francis, *ego confido in castallis Domini, idest daemonibus.* Even the devils are wardens of the Lord." Then, as Anna had asked earlier in the evening, seeing Vibeke draw something from beneath her apron, he inquired: "What have you there, Vibeke?"

"It is a flying rowan, Pastor. It has virtues against demons. If you would put it in your room, over your bed, it would let you rest without torment."

Sören smiled, for the first time that evening. "No, Vibeke, no," he said gently, being deeply touched at her solicitude. "That would avail me nothing."

"But did you not just say that this is a devil, that tries to anger you? This has power against devils. It was gathered on Ascension Eve."

The good woman leaned forward, holding out the little withered spray of mountain ash, beseechingly, and to her bewildered appeal the parson replied, ever more gently: "It is not in the power of any sprig, blessed or unblessed, to save me. It is only in the strength of my own spirit that I may be delivered from this devil, if devil he is."

"Ah," said Anna with a long sigh, "I still wish with all my heart that you would send Niels Bruus away. He is such a poor, dull-witted, worthless fellow to play the part of a demon."

The parson assented. "Dull he is, and poor. All the more reason, therefore, that I should withhold my anger from him. Perhaps I can never make you understand; but it is as plain to me as sunlight on the earth that I must keep him as my servant until the day he leaves me of his own free will."

Chapter Ten

He spoke with such firmness and such solemnity that neither of the women felt able to protest again. They sat in silence, greatly cast down in spirit, and it was the parson who broke the silence. His tone was lighter, as if he had greatly eased his own spirit by his declaration. "I thank you, Vibeke, for your care. I thank you greatly. Do you put the bit of rowan by your own bed. Although it has no power against my demon, it will, I am sure, be proof against the old women of Aebeltoft. Or of Skaane."

So Niels stayed on. He had become, in a way beyond his comprehension, possessed of an immunity as far as his master was concerned. He noticed, even he, that Sören Qvist, when speaking to him, had developed the habit of standing with his hands behind his back. He was aware that all rebukes for his laziness or his incompetence were tempered by a great patience. He received also many preachments, as he called them. The parson praised him, encouraged him, reasoned with him, and all of this which might have touched a man with some faint essence of nobility became for Niels but the license to conduct himself with greater impudence. He was in his own way bewildered, but since Morten, when these things were reported to him, rewarded Niels, and since the parson stayed his hand, and since Kirsten was pretty, although not always kind, Niels shrugged his shoulders and made the best of his days.

The growing season, compressed from either end, as it were, by the late northern spring, the early fall, was swift, and contained great drama for those who were concerned with it. It seemed a brief time from the day when the rye was tall enough to bow in the wind until the day when, heavy-headed, it was ready to be cut. The summer, cool and springlike, was in a few weeks the sunburned summer, with tawny haycocks and a strong pungent odor of herbs and grasses distilled in the heat. Then, with September, nearly every day brought its reminder of cold days coming. The storks went southward, trailing their long legs. Like the piled snowy cumulus of summer, they lifted the eyes of the farmer above the treetops to the wideness of the sky, and were a warning that the good days were not forever.

Judge Thorwaldsen was urging Anna to set the date of the wedding, and had once almost held her committed to the week of Martinmas. He had courted faithfully and well, and she no longer held him off because she wanted to hear him plead. She was in love with him, as he with her, deeply and happily, and the hope of adventure which had thought of journeys to Aebeltoft or even to the King's Copenhagen was all absorbed in the adventure of finding out how deeply she was in love. But she refused him because of Sören. She felt that as long as her father continued in this strange duel with his servant, and as long as Niels persisted in staying on the farm, she dared not leave the old man. She had tried, as her father had indicated that he wished her to try, to explain to Tryg why Sören retained the worthless servant. She was no theologian, and she had not fully understood her father when he talked of devils

141

as the wardens of God, but she understood him by love and intuition in the essence of the matter. The parson could not let himself be abased by his servant. For any other reason he might dismiss Niels, but not because the servant had brought the master to anger.

The judge was a practical soul, and his thought was as simple and clear as his eyes. He did not understand the demons of the Lord, either, nor how Sören had put himself in a position of bondage to his servant, but he had great respect and affection for the old man. Still, when it became a question of waiting for his own marriage until Niels Bruus chose to leave the parson's service, he began to make suggestions of ways in which pressure might be brought to bear upon Niels. He even thought of speaking to Niels directly. But Anna begged her lover not to interfere. Although she could hardly say why, she felt that the parson would be well aware of any outside influence in the matter, and that this relationship between her father and his worthless servant had become so deep and destined a matter that it would work the parson spiritual harm to have it settled in any way other than the way he chose himself. So Tryg was forced to let the argument drop.

As for Sören Qvist, he saw the rose haws redden in the hedges and the hazelnuts grow round in their velvety green and tasseled wrappers, and knew them to be remarkable for their beauty. The daily struggle of his spirit bred a daily exaltation, and common things assumed great meaning. Water, when he bathed his face or drank at the well, was extraordinary for its wetness and coldness; food, partaken of at his own board or in the field; the strength of his white mare that bore him up so loyally; the darkness of the night sky that brought him rest—these things were all extraordinary for themselves, and, more so, for the greatness of the creation behind them. So that he was attended in those autumn days, not only by the demons, but by the glory of God.

The demons did not cease to torment him. He knew that although he held his hands behind him when he talked to Niels, and did not strike him, yet anger rose in his heart; and he hated the sight of the man as he had never hated that of any human being. This knowledge made him immensely sad. Merely not to strike was not the victory for which he prayed.

It was not the first time in his life that he had been beset by this extreme consciousness of the visible and tangible world being but the sign manual of its creator, but never so continually, nor attended by such a growing sense of anguish. He thanked God to be greatly occupied with his parish, with his sick and his needy. The year had been a good one for harvests. In midsummer the news from the south had been disquieting, telling of the King's mishap before Hamlin, when the scaffolding had broken above the moat and the King and his horse together had fallen thirty feet. The King had survived either by the extreme toughness of his constitution or because the stars had outlined other business for him to perform before his death, but the campaign had been seriously delayed by his disaster. Still, there was nothing yet to indicate that Jutland would in another two years be laid open to an invading army. The parson concerned himself with local business and his farm.

The first frost swept the beechwood lightly, turning some leaves yellow, so that under a cloudy sky it yet looked as if rifts of sunlight lay upon the trees. When the true frosts began, the woods turned pure gold, leaf by leaf. The grass was stiffened underfoot before the sun rose, and wilted and sere when the ice had melted from it. The frost began to bite deeper into the ground, and the parson, who had of late neglected the garden by the house, realized that the autumn spading must be accomplished within a day or two, or the ground would be too hard to cultivate. Contrary to his usual custom, for he liked to do all the work in the enclosed garden himself, he gave orders to Niels Bruus that he should thoroughly spade the cabbage beds and rake up the withered haulms and cabbage stalks. He explained to Niels why he wished the work done without delay, and went into his study to write his homily for the coming Sunday.

It had been an exceptionally busy week, and the coldness of the air had made him feel for some days perhaps unduly pressed about the unfinished business of the farm. He found it hard to turn from the consideration of his practical affairs to the composition of his sermon. But he began.

"Inasmuch as we are all servants of God," he wrote, with scratching pen. It was nearly noon. When he lifted the quill from the paper he could hear, beyond the two closed doors, the faint sound of the spade as Niels began his work in the garden. Somewhere a noonday cock crowed, and in the kitchen were the indistinct voices of the women of the farm. The parson began to write again. He should not have left the preparation of his sermon until so late in the week. He wondered if Niels in his slowness would be able to finish spading the garden before nightfall. If he did not, the parson would have to finish the work himself. Kale and cabbage were two things without which he could not get through the winter. They could grow in spite of the cold, if started rightly; he had many times shaken the snow from green kale.

While he was writing, the noise of the pen was loud and he could not hear whether or not Niels was still spading in the garden, and it troubled him that the consciousness of Niels, and the suspicion of him, should follow him even into his study and into the preparation for his Sunday. He laid down the pen and knelt for a short time in prayer, and all the time that he knelt he could hear the blows of the spade, irregularly, and reproached himself for listening. He took up the quill again, dipped it in ink afresh, and wrote, "For whosoever saith unto his servant, labor, and does not labor himself . . ." and then paused, while the ink grew dry on the tip of the quill, for he could not hear the spade. When the blows began again, reassured, he returned to his own labor.

This went on for a good half hour, a half hour of listening, of writing, and of self-reproach. But the thought persisted that the plot must be spaded, and that by daylight. The sermon could, at need, be completed by candlelight. At the end of the long half hour there came a longer pause than any so far, during which Sören Qvist could detect no sound of the spade. In double annoyance, with himself and with Niels, he rose from his desk, went into the passageway and thence into the garden.

The garden was windless and full of sunlight. On one side the white wall of the house caught the light fairly, and the thatch, weathered and yet golden, glowed like the straw stacks in the stubble fields. An open window at the far end, the only window in the wall, that of the servants' room, made a dark accent under the thatch. To the right, beyond the thick wall of leaves, rose the hillside with its masses of golden beech. The hazel bushes were tenacious of their leaves, although tones of yellow and umber had crept into their ranks. They yet stood in a wall that shielded the garden completely from the road. And the garden was empty. Toward the middle of it, in the partly spaded bed, stood a spade, upright in the earth. But there was no Niels in view. Sören, standing just outside the doorway from the house, considered the extent of turned earth and judged it to be little in consideration of the time spent. He heard voices beyond the hedge, at the farther end, and laughter, and then Niels pushed his way through the bushes. His hands were full of hazelnuts. He must have seen the parson, but he returned to the spade as if he had not noticed him and, leaning one elbow on the handle of the spade, proceeded to crack and eat the nuts which he had gathered. Sören, approaching him, said in some impatience, but not in anger, "Why art thou not working as thou wast told to do?"

Niels, lifting his eyes from the nuts in his hand and smiling slyly at the pastor, replied: "I like better to eat nuts. Besides, it is not my work to dig in the garden. I am to work in the fields."

"Thou art to work where thou art bid," said Sören Qvist, his anger rising in spite of himself.

Niels shrugged his shoulders and rubbed his chin with the back of his hand.

"Thou art an ill-mannered dog," said the parson.

He had addressed Niels in the familiar speech which he used for the most part with his servants and his family. Niels, in replying, used it too, which was beyond his privilege.

"Parson," he said insolently, "thou art a rogue."

He pulled the spade from the earth with one hand, and with the other, having tossed away the empty nutshells, pushed back his battered hat as if the better to view the parson. He continued to smile, as if it gave him satisfaction to see the parson struggling with his anger, and there was security in his smile, as if he understood his immunity.

Sören Qvist stared into this smiling face, into the green eyes so strangely lighted; he saw the black stubble like a grime darkening the lines about the mouth and nostrils; he saw the tarnished leaden earring in the right ear. He saw them with a passion of hatred so great that his arm rose from his side, weightlessly, as if through water, and before he could check himself he had struck Niels twice in the face.

147

Niels shrieked and flung the spade violently to earth. He cried, in a loud hoarse voice which must have been audible in every room in the house, "Thou hangman! Thou rogue! Blackguard! Murderer!"

The last word rose upon the air in a shriek and hung there, and Sören Qvist, quite out of his head with rage, picked up the fallen spade and struck the man before him twice with the flat of the blade, crying out himself as he did so: "I will beat thee, yes, I will beat thee, thou dog, until thou liest dead at my feet!"

Niels fell full length to the ground, flat upon his face, and as he dropped, the fog of anger cleared from the eyes of Sören Qvist and he understood that he had been betrayed again.

As Niels had stood before him a moment since, smiling, he had been for the old man the absolute personification of all evil.

"I will slay thee!" Sören had cried, looking into the green eyes of Niels so curiously lit by that smile that they glowed with an infernal brightness. Now, as Niels lay upon the ground, he was become a man, a man in rags, in humble, perishable flesh. Sören bent over him in terrible fear, but the man was breathing. He was not even stunned. Passing his arm about Niels's shoulder, Sören helped him to his feet and, still with his arm about the man's shoulder, began with his free hand to brush the dirt from his clothes.

Suddenly Niels broke from him and ran across the garden to a spot in the southern hedge, away from the road, and there he parted the bushes and scrambled through the hedge. The parson saw him presently on the far side of the hedge, running across the upward-sloping meadow to the beechwood. When his dark shape had disappeared behind the screen of leaves, Sören Qvist sank to his knees and, covering his eyes with his hands, thanked God that he had not killed Niels Bruus.

"Blessed Lord and Master," he prayed in the quiet of the garden, in desperate humility, "deliver me at last from this temptation. Remove this man from my ways. Behold, I am not worthy of the trial. Forgive me that I thought to set my strength against his strength, who goeth to and fro in the earth, and walketh up and down in it, now even as in the days of the patriarchs. I have no strength, unless You give it me."

Here Anna found him, still upon his knees.

Chapter 12

On the second night following the parson's great anger, Kirsten did not sleep very well. She thought that the parson did not rest well either. Lying awake beside Vibeke, she thought she heard him moving about. The weather seemed to be changing. The down quilt felt too warm, and the girl was thirsty. She got up for a drink of water and heard the wind rising, noticed how relaxed and soft was the night air. As she returned to bed she caught a glimpse in the passageway of the green dressing gown and white nightcap of the parson, and her conscience pricked her in that she had sometimes flirted with Niels. It was not that she was fond of Niels, but that she was fond of flirting, and neither Lars Sondergaard nor Hans would give her a playful look. They were good sober servants, but both of them, she thought, must be nearly as old as Vibeke. Still, before she slept again, she wished that she had always looked the other way from Niels. She had not meant ever to abet him in his impudence to the master.

Chapter Twelve

Vibeke slept and dreamed, and cried out once in her sleep in terror. When they had told her that Niels had run away, she had answered merely that God should be thanked, and she hoped that he would never come back. They had all indeed been glad that Niels was gone. Nevertheless the sorrow that he had caused yet hung over the parsonage.

Some few days later—when she was asked about it weeks afterward Vibeke could not be sure on just which day—she had gone to Vejlby market, and there had met Morten Bruus. He had come up to her smiling and asked: "What news of my brother Niels?"

"I thought all the world knew by now that he has run away again," she answered tartly.

Thereupon Morten had manifested surprise, but had said nothing further. But the next week, on market day, her friends had come to her and said that Morten was telling it all around that Parson Sören had harmed Niels and was keeping him hidden. Vibeke had protested indignantly, and her friends had of course agreed with her that Morten Bruus was an evil-tongue, no less. But all week long people came to her with fresh reports of what Morten was saying, and by the end of the week the story was that Morten would have the law on the parson unless he produced his brother alive and well. The next word from Ingvorstrup was that Morten declared he would make the parson produce his brother "even if he had to dig him out of the ground."

Vibeke repeated these things to Anna, and both agreed to keep them from the parson, who was sunk in melancholy and seemed so strange to his daughter that she was more than ever concerned for him. The weather too was melancholy. Instead of the clear cold spell which the parson had anticipated, which would have locked the ground but left the noontide sunny, the days were wet or foggy, and the brick floors of the house seemed like stones from the well. The first weeks of October passed, the parson remote and sad, his household hushed and apprehensive. Then the tide of rumors about the disappearance of Niels reached the parson's ears.

He did not reproach his family for their silence. But when he returned from Ida Möller's house, where he had learned what was being said of him, he went straight to his room and took from the inmost corner of his desk the leather bag in which he kept what ready coin the farm afforded. The bag was well known to his parishioners. In times of their distress he had drawn it forth and taken from it such small coins as might ease their difficulties. He put this bag now in his pocket, mounted his horse, and rode at once to Tryg's house in Rosmos.

"I have come to buy myself some peace of mind," he said, putting the leather bag on the table before Tryg. "You have heard, doubtless, what Morten Bruus is saying of me?"

Tryg acknowledged unhappily that he had.

"Then you must have a search made for Niels, and there is the money to pay for it."

Tryg made no motion to accept the money. "Morten's talk is the wildest nonsense," he said. "Who in this parish would take the word of Morten Bruus against yours? Niels has likely run away to join the King."

"I think so myself," said the parson earnestly. "He has many times told me that his brother would do nothing for him. One could hardly expect him to go to his brother for charity. But take the money, Tryg— there is not a great sum—and find out where he is, for it makes me unhappy to have such a thing said of me, even by Morten Bruus."

"As you wish it, Pastor," said Tryg. The old man turned to go, and Tryg rose and went with him to the head of the stairs. "There is no man in Vejlby parish so greatly loved as you are, Parson Sören," he said. "Slander cannot touch you. And I, for one, am glad the rogue is gone." He would have said further that he felt himself honored in that he would soon be the parson's son-in-law, but there was something so lonely in the parson's expression, as he turned to say good-by, that the younger man forbore to mention his own happiness. Sören Qvist went slowly down the stairs.

The parson had not been gone from Rosmos a full half hour when Judge Thorwaldsen had other visitors. The first of these was Morten Bruus himself. He was followed by a young laborer and by a stout middle-aged woman and by her sturdy fair-haired daughter. The judge thought he recognized all three as parishioners of Sören Qvist. They stood in a deferential and not happy group behind Morten Bruus and waited for him to make known his errand. Morten advanced to the edge of the table and, bowing slightly to the magistrate, said, "Sir Judge, before I mention my more serious errand, may I congratulate you on your approaching marriage?"

The judge checked his surprise and his resentment, kept his lips closed, and acknowledged the question, and dismissed it, with a gesture of the hand. Morten smiled a little and turned toward his companions.

"I have brought," he said, "these witnesses to support me in the charge which I am forced to make. You will remember, I think, Jens Larsen, of Vejlby, and the Widow Kirsten, widow of the former shepherd of Ingvorstrup, and Elsa, her daughter. These are honest people, I think you will admit?"

"I have not questioned their honesty," said Tryg. "And your charge?"

"I charge the pastor, Sören Jensen Qvist, with the murder of my brother, Niels Bruus."

"I have heard that the charge has been made informally about the parish," said Thorwaldsen very gravely. "It is a serious thing to make it formally, to me, but it is better that it should be made openly, and now, so that it may be openly refuted."

Morten gave a short, hard laugh. "It cannot be refuted until it is brought to trial," he said.

"It cannot be brought to trial," said the judge sharply, "until there is more substance to the charge than I have yet heard of."

"You have not heard my witnesses," retorted Morten. "I demand that you hear my witnesses. I demand justice, even from you, Sir Judge." He leaned forward as he spoke, one hand on the table, and leveled at Thorwaldsen a long look of absolute malice and personal challenge.

Thorwaldsen felt the blood rising in his head, but he did not speak, nor clench his fist, nor let his eyes waver under the intense regard, until the accuser dropped back and, turning away, made a slight gesture toward the folk he had brought with him. These were watching in evident alarm, the girl especially in fear and the laborer Jens Larsen in distress. The Widow Kirsten let her eyes stray toward the leather bag which Sören Qvist had left upon the table, and Tryg, following her glance, remembered the reason for the parson's visit.

"As you may have guessed," he said quite calmly, and unhurried, "the parson has been here, even within the hour. He has left money with me, all that he has, I think, with which to search for Niels. He would hardly do that if he were guilty as you charge. Consider carefully, Morten Bruus, before you press this matter. It will go ill with you if the charge prove to be false."

"It would be money well invested for the parson," returned Morten, "if he could find my brother still alive. My witnesses, Sir Judge. Examine my witnesses."

He nodded to the widow then and took a few steps away from the table. He even walked over to the leaded windows and looked down into the street, as if to indicate his entire confidence in the testimony which these three people might bear. But when the widow began to speak, he turned and drew quietly closer.

"I wouldn't wish to say anything to harm Parson," said the Widow Kirsten, withdrawing her glance from the worn leather pouch before the judge, "for God in heaven knows that he has been kind to us, but I did once say that we heard him quarrel with Niels, Elsa and I. There's not much harm in that, is there?"

"Not much harm, and not much news, in that alone," said Tryg dryly. "But tell your story."

The widow folded her hands on her stomach and began as if she had told the tale many times before and were sure of her facts from much repeating of them, if for no other reason.

"About the hour of noon we were passing, Elsa and I, along the eastern side of the parson's garden, and as we were passing the bushes parted, and Niels Bruus looked out and offered some nuts to Elsa. While we were talking and eating the nuts, I heard a door slam somewhere in the house, and Niels nodded at me and winked. 'Stay and listen,' said he, 'and you shall hear a preachment.' Then he went back through the hedge and in a moment we heard the parson's voice. Then he scolded Niels for laziness, and Niels was impudent to the parson. Yes, he called the parson a hangman. Then the parson called Niels a dog, and he said, his very words, 'I will beat thee until thou liest dead at my feet.' Then we heard two blows struck as it were against a man's back, and we saw part of the handle and the iron blade of a spade swung twice high in the air. We saw this over the top of the hedge. We could not see through the hedge. Then everything was quiet and we came away quickly by the road. That was noon of the day that Niels ran away. Yes, Niels said to us, 'The parson has ordered me to dig, but I like better to eat nuts. Stay a minute, and you shall hear a preachment.'

Yes, yes, that was all, was it not, Elsa? And I don't see how that can do the parson harm." She finished, and stood breathing rapidly, as if she had just climbed a steep flight of stairs. Tryg considered her reassuringly.

"No," he said at length. "That is no more than what the parson himself has told us. There is no hanging matter there."

"One moment," said Morten hastily. "I have another witness here."

Jens Larsen spoke less easily. The words came hard; the man was unwilling and unhappy, but he began, "I was coming home late on that night, coming home from Tolstrup——"

Tryg interrupted him. "On what night?" he asked. "The night Niels ran away?"

"No, Sir Judge," said Larsen, "not that night. The second night after the day when, folks say, Niels ran away. Well, I was coming late from Tolstrup on the road that runs by the pastor's garden, and it was bright moonlight, although the wind was rising and it was not long after that we had the rain. I came by the garden and I heard someone digging, and it was very late at night. I was startled at first, as you might guess, and then I wanted to know who it was that was digging so late, so I took off my wooden shoes and I climbed up on the stile in the hedge. There I looked over, and I could see the parson leveling the ground with a spade. It was certainly the parson. He had on a green dressing gown that I know, and a white nightcap, and the moon was very bright. His back was toward me. Well, I wanted to see more, but he started to turn round, and

I did not like to be caught watching. So I climbed down softly, and took my shoes in my hand, and came away."

"There!" cried Morten suddenly, leaving the judge no time to consider this strange evidence. "There! It is plain to any what the parson was doing that night. Search the garden!" He came close to the table and beat upon it with his fists, and his voice rose until it approached a scream. "Search the parson's garden. There you will find the last witness to my charge!"

The parson had gone directly home after his visit to Rosmos. He had felt, in delivering to the judge his bag of money, that he had turned over to the law the practical responsibility for finding his missing servant, and the weight on his heart was a great deal lightened thereby. The moral responsibility for the disappearance of Niels he still carried with him, and was saddened by it, but the immediate question of what to do about Morten's slander had, he felt, been taken care of. He was almost happy, therefore, as he jogged along through the smoky autumn countryside. He rubbed down the mare himself, upon his return, and then paused in the kitchen to speak with Vibeke on casual matters, as he had not done in weeks. He was therefore still in the kitchen when Morten Bruus, accompanied by his witnesses and Judge Thorwaldsen, rode into the courtyard.

The two women had ridden pillion behind Morten and Jens Larsen. Tryg was on his own mount, and the three horses made no small clatter as they arrived.

Chapter Twelve

The parson stepped to the kitchen door to see what the commotion was about. Upon sight of the pastor, Morten fairly flung himself from his horse and, running forward almost to the doorway, cried in a loud voice: "There he is! There is the murderer of my brother!"

The maid Kirsten, starting from the dairy, stopped short in her tracks in alarm. Vibeke, also, ran to the kitchen door, and halted there as the pastor took a few slow steps forward toward his accuser. The women of Morten's party, having dismounted, still hung back, and Larsen made it his business to hold the two horses. Thorwaldsen looked about for Hans or for Lars Sondergaard, and called aloud for them, and Morten cried again, in a hoarse voice: "Murderer! I have come for the body of my brother Niels."

While the parson in bewilderment still looked down upon this violent figure without offering a word, Morten darted past him to the doorway and there tried to push past Vibeke, who spread her arms akimbo and blocked the way.

Thorwaldsen, meanwhile, seeing Kirsten, sent her in search of the men, and Morten's bay mare, unexcited by the cries of her master, trotted across the courtyard to where Larsen waited with the judge's horse and his own.

"What is the meaning of all this?" inquired the parson as Thorwaldsen approached him finally.

"The meaning," cried Morten, spinning about, "is that we have come to search your garden."

"I am sorry, Pastor Sören," said the magistrate. "He

demands the right to search and I must grant it to him."

"But search then," said the parson mildly.

"I must have a spade," said Morten.

"I will bid Hans to bring you one," said the parson. "Let him enter, Vibeke."

But Vibeke, feeling a touch upon her shoulder, had turned to find Anna just behind her, and pushed the girl back gently toward the spinning alcove as Morten rushed past them. Thorwaldsen followed him, and both were so intent upon their going that neither saw the girl shielded by the housekeeper. The parson followed more slowly, accompanied by Hans, and Vibeke and the other women came last of all, but one by one they issued into the quiet garden, until the whole of the accusing party and all of the parsonage servants were there.

Morten, taking the spade from Hans, ran into the middle of the garden and began to dig. The Widow Kirsten began to explain to Vibeke, in a whisper, that she meant no harm to the parson and that the magistrate had promised her that she had done no harm, but the silence of the others was so portentous that after her first sentences she fell quiet too. Morten dug with a fury, flinging the dirt recklessly upon the newly set-out plants. After a few minutes he ran to another spot and began to dig there, and then, finding the ground too hard, he moved to still another spot.

"This is strange behavior," said Sören Qvist.

Presently Morten approached the group, his face sweaty from the violence with which he had attacked the earth, and his eyes gleaming.

Chapter Twelve

"I cannot think," said Sören to him mildly, "what you will gain by all this labor."

"Ah, I shall gain plenty, never fear," returned Morten, and then, calling upon Jens Larsen, he said, "Show us now the very spot where you saw the parson digging upon that second night after the disappearance of my brother."

"I digging in the garden, and at night?" said the parson. "I was never out of bed the night after Niels ran away, nor the next, nor digging in the garden any night."

"We shall see," said Morten with a leer.

Larsen looked at the parson in apology, then crossed the garden to the stile. From there he looked back and selected a spot, then crossed directly to it.

"It was here," he said, "that I am sure I saw the parson working."

The place he indicated was littered with dried haulms and cabbage leaves. Morten approached it, spade in hand, and, looking down, remarked: "A likely spot. It has been well hidden."

"It has not been touched this season," said the parson.

"Well, shall I dig, Parson?" said Morten Bruus.

"Dig by all means," said the parson. "Or, if you are fatigued, ask Hans to dig for you."

Hans came forward then and cleared the rubbish from the ground. The watchers, pressing closer, saw that earth appeared to have been disturbed, especially in comparison with the earth near by, where little spears of green had started up. Hans made no com-

161

ment, but began to dig. The earth was soft, and yielded easily. Morten watched him, leaning forward in ever-growing excitement. Then suddenly Hans cried out: "God help us!"

They all drew a little closer, and Judge Thorwaldsen, coming right beside Morten Bruus, looked down into the hole, which was by then nearly three feet deep, at the spot where the shovel had last struck. To his great horror, he saw what was unmistakably the crown of a man's felt hat.

Morten cried out, "That is Niels' hat! I should know it anywhere! Ah, we shall find him, we shall find him! Dig away, Hans." Then, leaping into the hole, he began to clear away the dirt from the hat with his bare hands.

It was not long before he was able to pull the hat from the earth. He tossed it from the hole, and there was revealed the back of a head thatched with straight black hair. Still working furiously with his hands, having crowded Hans from the pit, Morten uncovered the shoulders of the corpse, which must have been interred face down, the knees doubled under it, and at last dragged it from the earth and stretched it on the garden path before the feet of Sören Qvist.

The parson had turned very pale. Vibeke, also, had grown white to the lips, and beads of cold dew stood on her fair skin, but she did not lessen her protecting hold upon Anna, who, standing beside her, had buried her face in the housekeeper's shoulder.

The dead man lay on his back, the lank hair falling freely to the earth. The face was so battered that not a feature was recognizable, and all the flesh was horribly far gone in decay. The stench from it, like that from an enormous dead rat, spread upon the sweet damp air. The body was fully clothed in the garments which Niels had worn on the day of his disappearance. Mudstained and limp, it resembled a scarecrow fallen from its stake, more grotesque than human. Morten, kneeling beside it, wrenched at the collar and turned out the neckband of the shirt, in which the name of Niels Bruus had been written. He pointed out the single leaden earring, and he called upon all those who were present to testify that this was the body of Niels.

One by one the servants of the parsonage came forward and gave their testimony. The maid Kirsten, having looked and nodded, clapped her hands to her mouth and ran weakly from the garden. The Widow Kirsten, horrified and amazed, gave her word that this was the body of Niels, and so did her daughter Elsa. Jens Larsen refused to testify concerning the identity of the corpse. He had not known Niels very well. Anna was excused from testifying, and Vibeke, having given her testimony with a nod, like Kirsten the maid, was permitted to lead Anna within doors. The parson stood his ground through all this, wan as he was, until each had spoken and withdrawn to the farther side of the garden. When there were left by the side of the corpse only Morten Bruus, the judge, and the pastor, Morten turned to the judge with his demand, and Thorwaldsen, to the pastor, said: "My dear sir, it grieves me to the heart, but I am left with no other choice than to put you under arrest."

The Trial of Sören Qvist

The parson's voice was very low, but firm, and he spoke directly to Tryg Thorwaldsen as if there were no one else in the garden. He said: "Before God, I am innocent of this dreadful deed. Surely this must be the work of Satan, or of his ministry. I have known for long that I was pursued of the devil. But He still lives Who will at His pleasure make clear my innocence. Take me to prison. In solitude and chains I will possess my soul and await what He in His Wisdom shall decree."

They took Sören Qvist to the jail at Grenaa, Anna riding with them because she would not leave him. The parsonage was left in a turmoil. Nevertheless, in spite of the excitement and confusion, before nightfall certain things were accomplished. Hans and Lars Sondergaard had made a wooden coffin and had placed therein the rotting body. The pit in the garden had been filled and the garden beds made orderly. Since Vibeke would not permit the coffin to remain at the parsonage through the night, the two men placed it on a barrow and carried it to Vejlby churchyard. Kirsten filled her milk pails as usual and took them to the dairy, and when darkness closed down upon the countryside, all the parsonage servants gathered in the kitchen, and Vibeke had supper prepared for them.

"This is as unpleasant a day's work as ever I did," said Lars, blowing upon his soup.

Kirsten looked at her bowl and did not touch it. "It spoils the taste of the food," she said. "I still feel sick."

"Who would have thought it would fall out like

165

this?" said Lars. "Niels to have been lying dead in the bushes those two days and none of us suspecting."

"What do you mean?" said Vibeke sharply.

"Well we heard it all," said Lars, laying down his spoon. "Just as the Widow Kirsten said. Didn't we, Hans?"

Hans nodded glumly.

"You never heard that Niels was lying dead in the bushes," said the housekeeper.

"We heard every word of the quarrel—like as you did yourself. We were mending old harness in our own room. The window was open. I wasn't looking out, but I heard everything—the cursing, and the blows with the spade, and then a rustling in the bushes, and then everything falling still. So it must have been then that parson hid the body, in the bushes."

"Niels broke through the bushes and ran away to the hill," said Vibeke.

"Who saw him run?" said Lars.

"Parson saw him go. It is natural that Widow Kirsten and her Elsa saw nothing more of him. They were on the other side of the garden."

"Well?" said Lars, shrugging his shoulders.

"Well, if Parson said that he ran and that he saw him run, that is true. Never would the parson tell an untruth."

"He is as good an old man as ever I knew," said Lars, "but I think even Parson might tell a lie to save his neck from the gallows."

"From the gallows indeed!" cried Vibeke. "From

the sword, rather. What kind of a shame do you wish upon the parson?"

"From the sword then," said Lars, "and all the more reason for fear. I am very sorry, Mistress Vibeke. In God's name, do not think I hold it against the parson. The life of Niels Bruus was never worth his. But what else can you make of the story of Jens Larsen? And how else came the body into the garden?"

"Ah, Jens Larsen," said Vibeke. "You ask me to take his word against that of Parson Sören?"

"The story of Jens Larsen is true," said Kirsten, and she told them how she had been wakeful on that night, and of how she had seen the parson in his green dressing gown and white nightcap, very plainly, because of the moonlight in the garden, and of how she had heard the door creak some time later when he returned.

Vibeke regarded her with wide and horror-stricken eyes. "It still cannot be true," she whispered. "It cannot be true."

"I hope you do not think me a liar," said Kirsten, weeping more bitterly.

Vibeke looked at her helplessly. Then, "No," she answered slowly, "no, I would not think so badly of you, Kirsten, but you might have been deceived."

" 'Twas bright moonlight," said Hans, speaking for the first time.

"Ah, you are all against him," said Vibeke in the deepest woe.

"I wish we might change matters," Lars Sondergaard replied. "Believe me, I would as soon run away tomorrow as testify against him, but at least I shall bear witness to nothing more than he himself has said before us all."

"I wish I had not said a thing," said Kirsten. "I will say nothing at all tomorrow about waking in the night, if the rest of you will not tell on me."

Vibeke looked from face to face, and saw no enmity. But no one spoke. The two men looked to her, and she answered slowly and unwillingly, "Best tell all the truth. Whatever is wrong will come right soonest with the truth. We are all bid to testify tomorrow at Rosmos, and running away will do no good."

They were still at their supper, but wordless, when Anna returned. She came into the house alone, having said good night to Tryg outside the door, and she sat down in her accustomed place at the table without having removed her cape. Vibeke had risen when her young mistress came in, but did not speak. The others looked to Anna as if for some announcement, and then looked back at their food as if they feared to distress her by watching her. She made no sign of greeting to them, but sat quite still, almost as if she had forgotten where she was or why she had come there. Her eyes went slowly from face to face, but so curiously unchanging in expression that Vibeke was frightened. Then Anna said quietly, "You have been weeping, Kirsten. You must not weep."

"Do you not bring us a message from Parson?" said Vibeke, at that.

Anna looked at her. "He says we must all be brave and trust in God," she answered.

"Why, that is right," said Vibeke, taking heart

again. "Do you hear? All is not lost. We are too easily cast down. Take off your cloak, Anna, and I will bring you some supper."

The girl shook her head. "I cannot eat," she said, rising to her feet. "I do not think I can sleep." And with no further good night she left the room.

Goodhearted Kirsten pushed away her bowl and, laying her head on the table, cried then as if she would never be able to stop. But Vibeke, having recourse to her chest of herbs, brewed a strong infusion of valerian and took it to her mistress in the Bride's Room, and stood over her until she drank it. She helped Anna into bed and sat down beside her.

For a while the girl lay trembling, but gradually the covers grew warm about her, the brew began to take effect, and she relaxed. Still Vibeke sat beside her, although the room was cold. At length Anna said, "Vibeke, I cannot understand it, and it makes me afraid. You know that there will be those who will think that he did it."

"There are always evil minds," said Vibeke.

"But of course he could not have done it."

"Since he said not," said Vibeke. "What does Judge Thorwaldsen say about it all?"

"I asked him only one question," said the girl. "I asked him whether he would take my father's word for the truth, and he said that he would."

"Then we should not be afraid," said Vibeke.

"No," said the girl, "we should trust in God, as he tells us. I am not really afraid, Vibeke."

But Vibeke was frightened. Long after Anna had

fallen asleep, she sat beside her as she had sat when Anna was little, after her mother's death, lest the child wake and cry out in terror. She did not doubt the parson's innocence, but neither did she see how the court could disregard the mass of evidence accumulated against him. She remembered what he had said of demons, and she began to formulate her own cloudy theories. Sitting there beside her sleeping child, she remembered things, dreadful things, which she had for many years put far back in her mind and had tried to keep there, overlaid by the many happy hours. It was late when she lay down beside Kirsten.

The gathering at Rosmos was small, and the witnesses only those whom Morten Bruus had brought there with him on the previous day and the members of Parson Sören's household. The parson, brought from the jail at Grenaa at early morning through the yet misty fields, wore still his farm clothes as on the day before, the leather coat and yellow cloth stockings and wooden shoes. His face was tired, like that of a man who has wrestled all night with an angel and yet been forced to let the angel go without receiving his blessing. There was dignity in his bearing, nonetheless, that made all those who were present doubly aware of his sacred calling.

Judge Thorwaldsen appeared last of all, took his seat at the long table, and began almost abruptly his examination. Morten's charge, and the testimony of his witnesses, the testimony of the parson's household, was just as on the day before, but on this day all statements were recorded by the clerk and made permanent. When the maid Kirsten told her story of seeing the green robe and white nightcap of the parson by the bright moonlight in the passageway, the eyes of Morten Bruus glittered with delight, and the parson was seen to pass his hand before his eyes. She was the last witness, and when she had finished, Morten Bruus sprang to his feet.

"The case is complete, Sir Judge," he cried. "I demand a sentence."

"Wait," said the judge. "The accused must have the opportunity to speak. Parson Sören Qvist, what can you tell us in your own defense?"

"So help me God," said the old man, speaking very slowly, "I will tell you only the truth. I struck Niels Bruus with a spade, and he fell down, yet he was able to leap to his feet and run away. I saw him cross the meadow and enter the woods. What became of him afterwards I do not know, nor how his body came to be buried in my garden. As for the evidence of those who saw me in the garden on that night, it is either a foul lie—and God forgive me if I accuse them wrongly —or a delusion of the Evil One. For I slept soundly on that night, and could not foresee what snares would yet entangle me round. Unhappy man that I am! I have no one on earth to speak in my defense—that I see clearly. If He in Heaven likewise remains silent, I have only to submit to His inscrutable will."

Anna, leaning against the arm of Vibeke Andersdaughter, thought that her heart had stopped with her breathing in the long pause that followed the parson's speech. Her father did not look at her as he sat down and covered his face with his hands. Tryg Thorwaldsen had not taken his eyes from the figure of the prisoner. In a voice that was no more than a whisper, yet loud in the silence, Morten Bruus repeated: "A sentence, Sir Judge."

Still Thorwaldsen delayed to answer, picked up a pen, and laid it down, folded and unfolded his strong, bony hands. At last he caught the eye of the clerk, nodded to him very slightly, and began to speak.

"Considering the good reputation of the prisoner," said Judge Tryg Thorwaldsen, "the nature of his calling, and the long period of service to his parish, and considering that his testimony is at variance with the testimony of other witnesses, the Court declares the evidence to be inconclusive. The Court cannot pass a sentence. However, the weight of testimony against the prisoner is such that it cannot be disregarded. Therefore the Court declares a three weeks' postponement of this case. At the end of such time, the Court shall reconvene in this town and at this hour."

The three weeks' postponement set the second hearing upon Martinmas. Judge Thorwaldsen was not aware of this, however, at that moment.

Late in the afternoon of that same day when the first hearing of the parson's case was held, the body disinterred in his garden was committed to holy ground in Vejlby churchyard, under the ministration of Peder Korf of Aalsö. Morten Bruus was there as witness and mourner, and Judge Thorwaldsen as the King's representative. In order to avoid the pile of unheaved earth, these two stood unwillingly side by side. Peder Korf took his position at the head of the grave, the sexton stood at the foot. Under the clouded sky the freshly turned earth, glazed where the spade had cut it, shone with a wan reflection, and the thick grass where the dew had gathered early gave off a like pale sheen. This twilight silveriness did not reach down into the deep rectangular hole. Morten appeared to be very sad, for once with neither malice nor mockery in his foxlike face. The judge, observing him, tried to grant him the honest right to mourn, but the recollection of his apparent lack of affection for his brother, and the sharp gleam of triumph which had kindled in his pale eyes when he had laid the outstretched corpse before the feet of Parson Sören Qvist, intruded on the moment and nullified the good impulse. In spite of himself his personal hatred of the man beside him filled his mouth with the bitter taste of gall.

Peder Korf read the words that blessed the dead, the sexton stood with his head bowed, his hands folded reverently upon the handle of his spade, and Morten Bruus covered his eyes with his hand. Tryg Thorwaldsen said within himself, "God forgive me." Behind them the church cast a great cold shadow; already old and destined to become much older, it held a tremendous stability. The words the parson was reading held the same stability. For Tryg Thorwaldsen they sealed the rotting flesh within the wooden coffin unto the great judgment. Whatever poor Niels had contributed to the situation in which his master was now placed, he was now beyond the judgment or blame of any human court. Whether absolved or pardoned, he was at least removed. The story of Niels was over, thought Tryg as the parson closed the book and the sexton lifted his spade.

Morten Bruus thanked the parson and bowed soberly to Tryg. He seemed disposed to linger at the graveside until the sexton should have completed his task, but Parson Korf and Judge Thorwaldsen turned aside and made their way through the narrow paths, between the resting places of earlier comers to this community, to the gate. As they quitted the churchyard, Tryg, looking back, saw Morten still standing with bent head beside the grave.

Chapter Fourteen

"Poor fellow," said Parson Korf. "It is hard to leave one's last living kin. Although there seems to have been but little graciousness between those brothers, yet the ties of blood are strong."

"It is the fate of the living that concerns us now," said Tryg.

"Even so," said the parson. "I am very sorry for you," he added quite simply.

"I should like to ask your advice," said Tryg. "Before Morten Bruus made his accusation, Parson Sören came to me, bringing a certain sum of money with which he thought I might conduct a search for Niels. What can I best do with that sum to help him now?"

Peder Korf tugged at his beard. His face was very brown and sunburned, his eyes blue, and from his sundarkened face his eyes looked at Tryg, seeming the more discerning for their intense blueness.

"You do not believe him guilty, then, Sir Judge?" he said.

"I cannot believe," said Tryg, "that he would stand before me and enact so monstrous a lie as to bid me search for Niels if he knew all the while where Niels lay. He is an honorable man, and a man of God."

"He is my friend," said Peder Korf. "Still, he is human, and all men are corruptible. He has always had the kindest of hearts. But anger riseth like a fire. It is quick and deadens the brain."

"Had I been convinced of his guilt, I should have passed sentence upon him this morning," said the judge.

"You think, then, that God may raise up a witness

to clear our friend? Offer a reward for a witness, then. But tell me, had not Pastor Sören another child, a son?"

"Yes," said Tryg. "A son Peder, who left home a great while ago. They believe that he was killed in Skaane."

"Yet perhaps he was not killed. Could you not, with the money, begin a search for Peder Qvist?"

"But he would be of no use as a witness," said Tryg.

"No," said Parson Korf, "but he would be a comfort. To tell the truth, I am afraid there is no witness who can help you."

A pause fell between them. Then the parson, very kindly, said, "My son, it is a great misfortune for Sören Qvist that you are the magistrate who must be responsible for his case. As the King's representative, your personal faith in Parson Sören can avail you nothing."

"Would it be better," said Tryg steadily, "if I were to withdraw from the case and ask that one of the King's traveling judges be asked to sit upon it?"

"I had thought of it," said Parson Korf.

"I too," said Tryg. "But a King's judge would be a stranger to this parish, and Parson Sören's reputation for goodness would have no weight with him. No, I'll keep the case."

"As you think wise," said Peder Korf.

"I shall need your prayers," said Tryg. Then, just as he was about to take his leave, "But consider, Parson Peder," he said, "is it not strange that Morten's accusation, leveled against the pastor only, brings to equal grief the three of us who have already felt his hatred—the pastor's daughter Anna, the pastor, and myself?"

At Vejlby parsonage Anna waited and hoped for a visit from Tryg, but he did not come, and she did not know why. She wanted to thank him for the postponement of the trial and for his public affirmation of his faith in her father's honesty, and she wanted to press him for a further promise never to let go that faith. She wanted also to feel her hands in his, that were so steady and strong. She thought that if she might only touch his hands the world in which she walked now might seem less full of quicksands, for in spite of her firm belief in her father's innocence and in Tryg's love and loyalty, she was terrified. She went about her household work as best she could, but from time to time Vibeke would find her seated, shivering, in the spinning alcove, her hands pressed between her knees, her shoulders bent, forgetful of whatever task she had set out to perform; and Vibeke herself was in no very confident frame of mind. The other servants went about their work quietly. They had all talked so much the day before that they were, for the time being, talked out. The hearing that morning had been a great excitement and strain, as well, and had left them all depressed and fatigued in spite of the fact that the magistrate had seemed to show himself a champion for the pastor.

Toward nightfall the bell in Vejlby church began to toll.

"That is a sad sound," said Vibeke, pausing at the opened door. "I do not like to hear it. It seems to say, 'Parson Sören is in prison, Parson Sören is in prison.'"

"It is the ringing for the dead," said Hans. "They have buried Niels Bruus."

"It sometimes seems to me the parson is as good as dead," Vibeke said with lowered voice. "But this Niels Bruus—why was he sent to plague us? Whenever we were rid of him he must needs come back, twice living and once dead. Well, now, as you say, he is buried in holy ground. He cannot rise to trouble us again."

She was very silent during the rest of the evening, so much so that even Anna, withdrawn among her own sad thoughts, became aware of it and forbore to speak to her. She made her preparations for the morning, for she meant to go the next day, taking food and clothing to her father in the jail at Grenaa, and as soon as her basket was packed and the kitchen made orderly, she withdrew into her own room. Here Vibeke came to her, as she was beginning to undress in the dark and cold. The housekeeper brought a candle and set it on the bride chest. Then she seated herself upon the other chest and folded her hands on her knee.

"You are extravagant," said Anna, unfastening her bodice. "I need no candle to go to bed by."

"I have something to speak of that needs a light," said the housekeeper.

"All that we have been speaking of all day," said Anna with a sigh, "needs a light, and that badly."

"I have been thinking," said the housekeeper, "and I know what must be done to save us. Judge Thorwaldsen must go, when a week is over, not sooner, with Parson Peder Korf, to Vejlby churchyard, and he must, by bright daylight, open the grave of Niels Bruus."

178

"Oh no!" cried Anna in horror.

"He must do that," said Vibeke firmly. "Then it will be found that the corpse is no longer the corpse of a man, but that of a cat, or maybe even only a bundle of rags, or a wax baby."

"And how should you know that?" said Anna gently, coming to sit beside Vibeke and laying her hand lightly on the hands of the older woman.

"Because I know the manner of witches," said Vibeke. Anna felt her shudder. Then she continued ever more firmly, "I know that they do such things as this. They enchant a bundle of rags to look like something else. They do it with the help of the Evil One. Let me tell you, for I know what I am talking about. It is as plain as day that Parson could not have killed Niels Bruus and buried him in the garden, for he said that he did not. Therefore the corpse from the garden could not have truly been the body of Niels Bruus. It was put there by a witch—never ask me who, but we shall know him—and it was made to seem like the body of poor Niels to us all. But now that it has been buried in holy ground, it will return to whatever shape it had before it was enchanted. Doubtless it has already changed, but for the sake of sureness we should wait one week, and let the holy bell ring above it more than once."

"Oh, dear heart," said Anna, "Tryg will never believe that, nor Pastor Peder either, and it is better to let the dead rest in peace."

"Let me tell you," said Vibeke, and her voice shook, "for I know about witches. They join a coven of which

179

the Evil One is the master, and they receive money from him as reward of their wicked doings; sometimes money, sometimes other things, such as jewels. And these shine very bright by moonlight, the gold coins and the jewels. But the next day, when the witch looks at her treasure, it will be changed into a little heap of dead leaves, or a handful of dung. This is the truth. You would think they would leave a master who tricked them so, but no, they work for the love of the evil they do, and the dung is as good a reward to them as the gold."

"I cannot think that this is true," said Anna. "Why are you always remembering these bad stories you have heard? They frighten you, and there is enough to be afraid of, God knows, without thinking of things that are not true."

"Oh, but, my child, they are true. Your father knows it. I know much more than I ever speak of. But if you will not believe me unless I tell you more"—Vibeke lowered her voice—"then I tell you that I once lived with a witch, and God help me but she was a wicked and a filthy creature, and her deeds almost cost me my life."

"My father says that trust in the Lord is the best protection against the spells of the devil," said Anna, alarmed by the fear which she saw in Vibeke's round eyes and by the way in which she trembled.

"I have never wanted to tell all this," said Vibeke, still in so low a voice that Anna had to bend closer to hear her. "I have been afraid lest the people of this parish learn of it and hold it against me, and I have wished to forget it, but now the time has come when you should know it, just as Parson knows it and your blessed mother did."

"Ah, don't speak of it, Vibeke, if it frightens you," said the girl. "Please don't speak of it."

"Yes, I must now," said Vibeke, "because if you will believe me, perhaps we can save Parson. You will keep it a secret, because you love me. It was when I was a girl in Aebeltoft. How should I have known, when I went to her as a servant, that she was a witch? But little by little I learned things. I was to help her dress and undress, and I saw the marks. At first I did not know what they were. Then I learned. I heard her talking to a toad she had. She would make a little chuckling noise, like a toad, and he would come, when she called him. She had another spirit too, a familiar in the shape of a little wild fox that sucked her. No, not at the breast, as a mother feeds her child, but at a teat in her side, and she fed it blood. Some of them have teats in their most private parts, as I have heard, but this one had hers under her arm, so I saw it. She was not a poor woman, no, she was rich, and well considered in Aebeltoft, until the trouble that betrayed her.

"Then she was brought to trial. I was afraid when I first knew that I was serving a witch, but I did not know how to leave her, for she had a paper. Then, too, I was afraid she would bewitch me if I left her. Had I run away, she would have known where I was hiding, and bewitched me. So even before they called her to trial, I suffered with her, and she made me do everything she wanted to, every kind of filthy work, and early, and late. I was only a girl, younger than you, and I was all the time afraid.

"Then came the trial, and at first I thought, I am free. Then some wicked person said that I must also be a witch. I had lived with a witch, it was said, and she must have taught me her bad art. When the wife of the burgomaster of the King's Copenhagen is burned for witchcraft, what can a poor serving girl expect? They do such things to make a witch confess, because it is known the devil hardens them against confession, that even to be accused is as good as to be believed a witch."

The cold sweat stood upon Vibeke's forehead as she spoke, and she turned her eyes toward the flame of the candle, as if the light of it did indeed give her courage to talk of these dark things.

"Then came your father," she said. "He was to be married to your mother at Aebeltoft where she lived, and when he heard of the witch trial, he came to talk to the judges. And so in some way that I have never understood, he persuaded them that the witch's serv-ant girl should not be tried with her mistress, but should be indentured to him and to his wife, and he would vouch for her Christian conduct so long as he and she should live. So I was spared the torture. And I was let help to dress your mother for her bridal, and I came with her to Vejlby to live, in peace and happi-ness."

Here the poor soul broke down and wept, and Anna wept also. Then Anna said, "And the witch?"

"She was burned," said Vibeke, drawing a long,

shuddering breath. "Now can you see why I am so sure that your father cannot be guilty of a great wickedness? And why I have loved your mother and her babies? And why I am afraid of witches? Oh, Anna, my little Anna, we must save Parson Sören, and I have told you the way to do it."

Chapter 15

Tryg's conversation with Pastor Korf in the churchyard at Vejlby left him no heart for a visit with Anna Sörensdaughter that evening. All through the grim afternoon he had cherished the thought of speaking with her; the tenderness of his thought for her was a charm against the malice and hatred which he felt drawing ever closer about them all. Yet when the moment came, when he had said good night to the pastor from Aalsö and he was free to turn to his love, the sense of his own predicament, which the pastor's words had made so plain, checked him at the familiar pathway and sent him comfortless home. He had hoped to comfort Anna; yet the assurance that he had already given her of his own belief in her father's innocence was all he had to offer, and this was now overshadowed by Peder Korf's warning. Whatever the sincerity of Tryg's loyalty, the world at large was sure to consider it founded less in his reverence for the old man than in his love for the daughter.

Once home, he set paper and ink before himself and tried to compose a letter by which he might express to

Anna, together with his love, the reason for his unwillingness to see her, but when he tried to speak of caution, it seemed like cowardice, and when he mentioned partiality it seemed an offense against his office, and when he tried to set forth the compulsion of the general opinion, it seemed a threat. In despair lest anything he write should hurt her more than his silence, he crumpled up his paper and threw it in the fire.

He was aware that had there been no question of Anna, he might have felt free to go against the evidence, and trust to his own conviction in the parson's adherence to the truth. Whatever he thought, his mind worked around in a circle, and at an hour's end he was at the point at which he had stuck that morning. However damning the circumstantial evidence, it still must be incomplete, for the parson's statement was also evidence, and it contradicted half of the other testimony. Therefore he must offer a reward for any witness who might bring further light to bear upon the case; and he would at the same time offer a reward for information concerning the whereabouts of Peder Sörensen Qvist. But what evidence did he hope for? That the testimony of Lars Jensen and the maid Kirsten be proved false? There remained the rotting body on the garden path. Who believed in the innocence of the parson, he asked himself, save only Anna, Vibeke, and himself? And was he indeed deceiving himself because of the power of his love? Had it not been well known since earliest times that all men were prone to believe that which they wished, and should he think himself exempt from the common failing of mankind?

With a groan he dropped his head in his hands, and saw before his darkened eyes the pale young face of his love. The eyes looked into his with trust, a child's trust, and yet, because of their sadness, a woman's too. So they had looked when he had last spoken with her, and would he dare ever to speak to her again?

He felt then that if he had, upon that fixed, approaching day, to pronöunce sentence of death upon Parson Sören Qvist, it would be no different from pronouncing death upon this girl; and that would be beyond his strength. There remained for him then only an appeal to the King to send another judge.

He lifted his head from his hands and saw before him the paper, waiting, and the pen beside it. He had only to write and be delivered from his responsibility. As the sense of his love grew, his doubt of himself grew also, until, in desperate tenderness and grief, he reached out his hand and touched the pen. He drew the sheet of paper closer. He dipped the quill in the ink and held it poised. And as he did so, there came the thought of Anna, waiting, to whom he would have to say, "I have delivered him, and you, to the mercy of a stranger, from whom I expect no mercy, because I could expect no mercy from myself."

"Then will not Morten Bruus look triumphant!" he said aloud to himself in the empty room.

He wrote no letters to anyone that night. With the thought of Morten Bruus came the feeling of being trapped, and he gathered all his energies together in the resolve to do his utmost to free the parson. In the morning he sent a servant to Vejlby to inquire after Anna's

Chapter Fifteen

health, and to say to her that he was kept from seeing her by his judicial business. It was Vibeke who received Tryg's messenger, for Anna was gone to visit her father.

The jail at Grenaa was a small building of two rooms, very strongly constructed of stone. In the outer room lived the jailer and his family. The inner room, in which the prisoners were kept, had no door save that opening into the outer room, but there was a little barred window set high in the wall. It was not customary for any prisoner to remain long in jail. The trials were brief and the punishment prompt, and for such humble and transitory sojourners the living accommodations provided were of the simplest.

By chance, upon that first visit, Anna found her father alone. The jailer admitted her without delay. He even apologized because the night soil had not been removed in some days, and called his wife to perform the task. But after that had been accomplished the place yet stank, and it was cold and dark. When the door had been locked behind her, Anna crossed the room to where her father sat on the edge of a low wooden bed and knelt before him. He lifted his hand to her head, then dropped it lightly to her shoulders and let it remain there, as if without strength. He was in chains, fastened to bands about his ankles. She waited for him to speak, but it was long before he did so. At last he said in the voice of a very old man: "It grieves me to see you in this place."

"It grieves me more to have to leave you here," she

said, and took his hand and pressed it to her lips. "But surely after the second hearing you will be released."

"No," he said, "I have such a sickness in my soul that tells me my God has forsaken me. I have given my life to His service. Why has He abandoned me? There is no comfort remaining to me save that I know here, in my own heart"—and he struck himself upon the breast—"that I am no murderer."

She tried to remonstrate, reminding him of Tryg's loyalty, of Vibeke's devotion, but he brushed aside all her reasoning. She had brought him food, the loaves that Vibeke had baked, and round sweet cheeses, and the drink that he himself had brewed, but he would have none of it. He begged her to thank Vibeke for her kindness, and he requested that his Bible be brought to him. Then he lapsed into a silence that he hardly broke to say good-by to her when the jailer opened the door and signed to her that she must leave.

When, on the following day, she gave him the Holy Book, he smiled at her, and she was able to persuade him to eat a little.

There began then for Anna a new routine of life which lasted all of the three weeks before the second trial. Every day she made the journey from Vejlby to Grenaa. She came to know the road as if it were the footpath from the parsonage to the church, the marshes where the sea birds came, the woods darkening to the east, and the wild heather country beyond. The jailer never permitted her to stay long with her father, but he was kindly toward her. On one cold day the jail-keeper's wife let her warm the beer at the small raised hearth of the outer room. Thereafter, when Anna had sometimes to wait before she could see the prisoner, she used to talk a little with the jailkeeper's wife. It was a strange thing to her to see the jail wife nursing her youngest in the red glow of the hearth, or to see her preparing food and going about the comfortable business of life while beyond the iron-banded door, just in the next room, waited so much sorrow and foulness.

One day some time after the parson's imprisonment, Anna saw crouched in the opposite corner of the inner room, upon a pile of straw, a young woman who kept her head bowed upon her knees during all the time of Anna's visit, so that she never saw her face. When she asked the woman of the jail about her, the woman answered only that she was a wench who had killed her baby within the hour it was born.

"She is to be beheaded," she added, looking curiously at Anna.

On the next day the young woman was gone, and in her place were two thieves who consoled each other by casting dice. Few other visitors were allowed in the jail, but the procession of miscreants came and went, some more unfortunate than others; and sometimes the inner room was crowded, and frequently it was empty save for the presence of Parson Sören Qvist. But the parson's reputation brought him at least this kindness, of having his daughter with him for a short time each day.

Anna made his bed, and bathed his face and hands, and brought him food, and all as if for a sick man. It seemed incredible to her that he should be so changed in so short a time. All the fire and vigor and geniality which had seemed so much a part of him were quenched, as if by the stifling air of his prison. The hand which his daughter touched was limp, and when he spoke it was only in a faint voice. He was very gentle with her and still showed his affection and concern for her. He daily lamented that she should be exposed to sights and odors of such vileness. To see him so broken was her greatest grief, and each time she left him the weight of her sorrow was such that she seemed to feel it laid across her shoulders like a heavy wooden yoke. Yet she walked bravely through the outer room and held her head up and her shoulders straight, and it was only in the safety of the bride bed at home that she let herself weep.

She had had Tryg's message from Vibeke, and then had heard no more from Tryg. Through the first week of his absence it seemed reasonable to suppose that he was indeed too busy to see her, and although she lacked him sorely, she was not unduly distressed on that score. But as the second week drew on, the fear began to visit her that Tryg avoided her because he had changed his mind regarding the parson's innocence. Vibeke did not cease to urge her to speak to Tryg concerning the opening of the grave.

"I cannot speak to him if I do not see him," said Anna.

"Then send for him," said Vibeke, and at length the girl yielded to the housekeeper's urging, and Hans was dispatched to Rosmos. He returned with a letter for Anna. It was written hastily, and while Hans waited.

Chapter Fifteen

Tryg begged her to believe that he was doing everything in his power to find some new evidence that might exonerate the parson. He had found it wiser not to visit her during this period. He assured her of his love and besought her to care for her health.

"That is all," said the girl to Vibeke. "You see, he will not come."

"Then I will go to him myself," said Vibeke.

"Let me talk first with my father," said Anna.

To know that someone was exerting himself in behalf of the parson gave Anna more courage and more hope than she had felt since she had parted with Tryg, and she tried, when she next saw her father, to convey her fresh hope to him. She told him of the judge's letter, making little of Tryg's unwillingness to see her, and much of his efforts to find a new witness. The old man listened to her with clouded eyes, and when she had finished repeated what he had said so many times before.

"There is but One witness who can save me, and if He remain silent, I am surrendered to mine Enemy. But He has withdrawn His kindness from me. I am treated as if I were indeed the murderer of my servant." He then added, in a voice of inexpressible weariness: "I know very well that I did not kill Niels Bruus. I cannot understand how his corpse came to be in my garden."

"Vibeke has an explanation," said Anna hesitantly. "She bade me tell you that the grave should be opened, and, now that the body has lain in holy ground, it will be found to have changed to a bundle of rags, or some

191

such worthless matter. She says that it was never a real body, but that some enchantment had only made it seem so. She says that it is the work of the devil, and she would name names but that she is afraid."

"Vibeke has suffered much," said the old man. "She has reason to be afraid."

"She wishes me to go to Tryg," said Anna, "and demand that the grave be opened."

The pastor made a negative motion with his hand. "No, no," he said, "do not go to Tryg with such nonsense; do not let yourself be troubled by Vibeke's tales. Nevertheless," he said, rousing himself, "there is the power of the devil in all this." His voice grew stronger, and his eyes, beneath the white overshadowing brows, clearing, burned dark and intent. "He is called the Slanderer and the Accuser, and hath both accused and slandered me. He is called the Adversary. He hath crossed my ways and set himself against me, and encompassed me with snares. Whether he tempt me in the shape of Niels or accuse me with the mouth of Morten Bruus, it is all one, for the struggle is here," and he struck himself above the heart. "Ah, it is bitter to think of death, but it is ten thousand times more bitter to feel that the Grace of God has departed from the heart. And what else can I feel, in my weakness and in my confusion?"

There came a day when Anna entered the jail to find the jailer absent and the jail wife entertaining by the hearth a burly man dressed in the plainest of clothing, leather jerkin and short leather trousers and wooden shoes, and having a short grizzled beard about a weathered countenance. The jail wife had given him hot beer and such cakes as her cupboard could afford, and he sat drinking with a sort of unaccustomed contentment. Anna set herself down upon a stool at a little distance from the hearth, and as she waited for the jailkeeper to return with his keys, she watched the man by the hearth. He talked little and, when he had finished his drink, looked as if he meant to leave at once, save that the six-year-old son of the jail wife came and stood by his knee. Their voices were low, and Anna hardly heard their small conversation, but she saw the man hunt in his pockets and draw forth a small gift for the child—she thought it was a copper—and then pat him upon the shoulder before he stood up to go. She did not know why he drew her interest, save that he seemed lonely; later she asked the jail wife who he was.

"Why, that is Villum Ström."

"And who is he?"

"Why, he is the executioner," said the jail wife in some surprise.

"And do you serve him drink, and drink with him yourself?" asked Anna in reproach.

"Why not?" said the jail wife. "There are few enough folk who will drink with the executioner."

Thereafter Anna thought of him often, at times with terror and then with pity, because she herself would not have cared to drink with him; and it was strange to her that the executioner should have a name, like other men. She wondered how much he was paid for the punishments he enforced, and whether he had been driven by great poverty to earn his food by the sufferings of his fellow creatures, or, if not, how and why he had taken up such a trade; and whether he might ever be released from it, and buy himself a farm or a fishing boat, and so become one with the men who earned their living without invoking cruelty. He had not seemed to be cruel in himself, nor depraved.

She thought also of the wretches who shared from time to time the parson's new habitation. She had known poverty among the peasants of Vejlby parish, and suffering among the old and sick, but she had never in her young life encountered the misery of sin and of retribution combined with the misery of poverty and illness. All these were in the jail at Grenaa. She had thought, during the early days of her father's imprisonment, only of her own tragedy and her father's unjust fate, and it came to her as if with surprise that there were other men and women in prison, and some on their way to death, all on their way to suffering and despair. It was another world of whose existence she had not dreamed in the security of the Vejlby parsonage.

Upon one dark afternoon she came hooded and cloaked to the jail through the dripping fog and the narrow cobbled ways where the half-timbered houses, for all they stood so close, were shuttered and unfriendly. The jailkeeper was again away, and she sat down to wait close to the hearth, where the jail wife had placed her stool. The little boy drew near her as she set her basket on the floor and arranged her skirts about her knees, and she smiled at him. He had a head of hair like thatch on a roof, straw-colored and straight and coming down thick over his eyebrows, and under this thatch his eyes were grave, and his wide, childish mouth was grave also, so that for a moment Anna wondered if the jailkeeper's boy, like the executioner, found few who would drink with him. So she smiled and held out her hand. He came closer and, standing by her knee, looked up into her face without speaking. But by and by he said: "Would you take off your hood and let me see your hair?"

It was not what she had expected. She had expected, if anything, that he might ask for a bit of one of the loaves she had brought for her father. The request seemed very simple and easily granted. She pushed back the hood of the dark serge cape and untied the white linen cap which covered her hair. Her hair was braided that day and bound smoothly about her head, save for little curled tendrils that escaped about her face and curled ever the more tightly because of the wet air. The light from the hearth shone upon this golden cap, chased with the little curved lines of the braids like the finest piece of goldsmith's work, and the boy looked and smiled.

In due time she replaced the cap, but not before she had had a vision of herself, sitting beside the hearth as the executioner had done, talking with the jailkeeper's child; and the fact that she had been bareheaded in this room, as if it had been her own house, gave her the feeling of having become one with the world that belonged in the jail. It had also become her home. Strangely, she did not feel that she had become degraded thereby, but that she had received a comfort deeply needed, the comfort of fellowship.

So the days went by, slowly enough in their sadness, but with a terrible relentlessness when their end was considered. The bony hollows in the face of Judge Thorwaldsen grew deeper, and the lines about the wide mouth were set and strained. In spite of his efforts he had discovered nothing which might help him out of his dilemma; neither was he willing to abandon the case to a stranger. He was cut off by his own integrity from the only two people from whom he might have asked comfort, and he had not even that alleviation of his loneliness which Anna Sörensdaughter had in her sense of kinship with the oppressed. He kept his solitary way, and people drew apart from him in the market places, partly because of the dignity of his office and partly because of his harassed and haunted eyes.

Anna had folded Tryg's letter small and kept it with her. It was the only letter which she had ever received from him, and in it he had said that he loved her. It became for her as the weeks went by more than an assurance of his love; it became the one security for her father's life. In her mind, which was simple and direct in its affection, Tryg's love for her meant that he could not destroy her father. At the end of the third week, on the eve of the second trial, she ventured to speak to the parson of this last, hoarded hope. He had grown very infirm in those three weeks; being still chained by the ankles, he had been unable to take any exercise at all; the good color had all faded from his face, and the flesh, as it seemed, had melted from his bones. His melancholy had grown upon him, and his apathy, so that at times he had seemed to his daughter remote beyond appeal. Though she had ministered to him daily according to her best knowledge, and had brought him daily her affection, she felt sometimes that he was a dweller in another world, whose body only remained in prison, who heard her only faintly when she spoke. Still, he was always gentle with her, and his eyes followed her when she left the place, so that she knew he wished her with him, and it broke her heart daily to leave him. He listened to her gravely when she spoke of Tryg.

"He refused once to condemn you," she said, "and he has no reason to have changed his mind. You will be free tomorrow, I am sure. You are too good and too kind to die like a common criminal."

"Do you think I should be happy, then," said the parson very gently, "to live under the shadow of so great an accusation? Ah no, if He who made us all will not exonerate me, I do not wish to live. To live without God's Grace is to be dead though living."

"I cannot think," said Anna, "that you who have lived so good a life should be without God's Grace."

"It is His to give or to refuse," said the old pastor. "Perhaps I thought once I could achieve it by feeding beggars. Now He reproves me for my arrogance. Oh, I have besought Him. Well, but we have not spoken of you."

"There is no need to speak of me," said Anna.

"There was to have been a wedding at Martinmas,"

197

said the old man. "I wish I might have seen you wedded before all this happened. It is a bitter thought that I, who love you almost more than my own soul's salvation, should be the cause of wrecking all your happiness."

"You must not speak as if everything were ended," she answered. "Tryg has been like a son to you. He will not let you die."

"I am not thinking of my death," said the old man, "but of your happiness. How can a magistrate marry the daughter of a criminal?"

"But Tryg will never condemn you," cried Anna.

"You trust him greatly," said the pastor, and his voice was sad.

"Why should I not?" answered the girl.

"Men change," said the pastor.

"But not Tryg," she said, half pleading, and felt, in spite of her trust, a coldness settle about her heart as her father replied, "Tryg is human."

Then he said: "You are grown very white. Believe me, I do not mean to be unkind. But I cannot leave you with no thought for your future, and my time is short. When have you last spoken with Tryg? Not since the day of my imprisonment. Nor have I seen him since my trial. You have a letter in which he speaks of the unwisdom of your meeting. His position is not easy. I cannot blame him. But do you not see how the wind is shifting?"

Anna bent her head and said in a voice that was almost a whisper: "I had thought he would love me always."

Chapter Fifteen

"So may he love you always," said the pastor, "but as a magistrate he may not wed you."

All her young life her father's wisdom and authority had been absolute. She found no answer now for what he told her, but sat with her head still bowed, and the parson, lifting his two hands to his face, prayed wordlessly. The silence which fell between them seemed long, for in the cold, shadowy room, shut off from the cries of the town, from all the activities of people or of living things, there was no motion by which time might be measured. Yet in this pause of time she had the increased consciousness that time was brief, and she heard again her father's voice saying, "My time is short."

She said at last: "I am sure we are wrong to despair," and at her voice the parson dropped one hand to hers but still sat motionless, with his eyes covered.

The door to the outer room was very thick, and the footsteps of those without were never heard within, nor their voices, but as Anna and the parson sat thus, quietly, the girl heard the lock grate as the key was turned, and thought: "Now I shall be asked to leave, and this is my last visit." The time which had not seemed to pass had gone, had come to an end.

Slowly the door swung inward, and the trembling gleam of a rushlight fell upon the stained floor. The jailkeeper came into the room. He was followed by another man, and fleetingly Anna thought that a new prisoner had come to spend the night with her father. But the jailkeeper stood to one side, his rushlight in his hand, and let the man who had followed him cross the room to where she sat with her hand enclosed in that of her father. The parson looked up; then stood up, swaying. He slowly put one hand upon the stranger's shoulder and turned him a little so that the light which the jailer held could shine upon his face. The stranger was young, and fair-haired.

"It cannot be," said the parson, "and yet it must be so, since I am wide awake."

"It is so," said the young man with a smile.

Then Anna saw her father put both hands upon the stranger's shoulders and drop his head upon one of his hands, and she knew that the stranger must be Peder Qvist.

Chapter 16

There had come a fisher's boat to Varberg in Skaane with a catch of herring. The young overseer of a manor some miles inland, being in the harbor town on business, came down to the docks to visit with the fishermen. He had made a habit of doing so for many years. He had talked to men from both sides of the Kattegat, from Norway, from the islands of Zealand and Fünen. Those who returned often to Varberg remembered him, and brought him news of their home ports. He was most interested in the news from Jutland. On this day early in November of 1625 the fishers had lately come from Grenaa, and their talk was largely of the trial of Parson Sören Qvist. Peder the overseer had got the entire story from them before he told them that he was the parson's son. They were much concerned on his account. Although not one of them had ever seen the parson, being not Jutlanders but men of Skaane, they had heard everything good of him; the popular imagination had begun to side with the pastor, the more especially as his case looked desperate; and they offered to take Peder to Grenaa. They might have been there a day sooner had not bad weather forced them to take refuge on the island of Anholt. Had the weather been as fair as they had hoped, Peder Qvist remarked with a smile, perhaps they would now be less good friends, but rain, wind, and delay had made them close companions. They had arrived at Grenaa this afternoon, as the dusk was falling, and he had come at once to the jail.

He had been a soldier in Skaane, as Vibeke had surmised, and had remained there, chiefly because he had married there and his wife had been unhappy at the thought of leaving her native parish. He had meant someday to come home, but there had always seemed some reason why he should not leave at the moment. He had heard of his mother's death, some months after the event, and that had in a way prevented his returning, for he had dreaded his father's grief and had been afraid that his desertion might be held up to him too bitterly. Peder was not eloquent save by his honesty and directness. He found it hard to tell his story. The very intentness of his audience distressed him. Yet it was evident that he was deeply thankful to have found his father still alive, and he made both Anna and the old man feel somehow, without his putting it into so many words, that his affection was as staunch as it had ever been, and that it had never been removed from them throughout his long absence.

The parson could not take his eyes from the face of his son. He had put his arm about Anna as she sat beside him, and as the young man spoke, haltingly, at times, yet always clearly and firmly, he tightened his arm about his daughter's shoulder as if he embraced them both. The change in his face was extraordinary. The great happiness suffused it as if with the color of health. The lines of strain, the darkness in the hollows of the eye was gone. It was such a change as comes in the face of a sick man when the fever breaks and a natural dampness and freshness comes upon the forehead.

He said, "God has answered the prayer of my heart," and his voice also seemed to have changed, regaining its old warmth. He said also, "What a comfort it will be to me this night to think of you sleeping at Vejlby! The very walls will be glad to have you back." He did not ask many questions, but seemed content to let Peder tell him such things as he would, of his fortunes, of his two children. When it was time to part, he blessed his son, Peder kneeling before him, and the large hand which had been so capable in its day rested lovingly upon the bowed, fair head. Peder Qvist, rising to his feet, smiled his quiet smile and, unashamed, wiped his eyes with the back of his hand.

When Peder Korf of Aalsö came late that night bringing the Lord's Supper to the old pastor, he found him in such an unwonted state of serenity that he was ready to believe the hurried whisper of the jailer as that humble man bent to unlock the door.

"In God's name," said the jailer, "he looks so well that I am sure they have found him a new witness and he'll be free on the morrow. I would risk money on it, I would."

203

But when Peder Korf had congratulated the prisoner upon his being prepared to take communion, and had repeated the jailer's comment, the old parson answered tranquilly, "God is my witness."

He then confessed himself to his friend, and was given the blessed bread and wine, and Parson Peder Korf again congratulated him, as was customary, upon his completing the communion, and added the hope that he would be strengthened by it for whatever might befall on the morrow.

"I am happier tonight," said Parson Sören with great earnestness, "than I have been in many a long month. My son Peder has returned to me, Peder, of whom you have heard, alive and well. Ah, it is not only the sight of him that gives me joy, but it seems to me tonight that my God has turned a loving countenance upon me. You cannot guess what I have suffered in these last weeks, feeling that all grace had been removed from me."

"It has all the look," said Peder Korf, "of a manifestation of divine kindness. God be praised."

"I am glad you think so," said Sören Qvist, and he went on to tell at length how it had happened that Peder should have returned, and where he had been, and how prospered. To all of the story Parson Korf listened with great interest and postponed the moment of his farewell. When at a late hour the jailer came to summon the visitor from the cell, and to add his congratulations piously to those already given by Peder Korf, Sören Qvist rose and said: "I thank you for your congratulations, and I thank you heartily for your visit. I wish that I might escort you to the door, but tonight I am still enchained." Then, looking from the man of God to the man of fetters and keys, he said, with a singularly happy smile, "I look for good fortune tomorrow. I do not know in what strange and unexpected form it may come, still I cannot doubt but that it will come, and that it will be from God."

"In God's name," said the jailer, and, "Amen," said Peder Korf.

 M ist lay on the fields that November morning as the party from Vejlby parsonage took the road to Rosmos. With them rode Peder Sörensen, a solid, fair-haired figure, firm in the saddle, and lending to them all, in his quiet young strength, a new security and hope. His father had been right: the very walls of the parsonage had been glad to see him, and Vibeke had laughed and cried until she hardly knew whether she were joyous or sad. She had been much distressed at the parson's refusal of her advice; that he refused to have the new grave in Vejlby churchyard disturbed seemed to her to be playing straight into the hands of the devil. She felt much as his father did about Peder's unhoped-for return: the kindness of God was in it. And now they were three who believed completely in the parson's innocence.

She followed him about the courtyard as he looked to see what had been changed in twelve years and what remained just as it had been, and followed him still with her eyes when, seated in his father's place at the table, he looked about the kitchen in mild astonishment to find each copper pot and pan still ranged as they had been when his mother was alive. After the meal she gave him minutely the domestic history of the farm in those twelve years, the story of every animal and every field, and the story of his mother's illness. She drew from him, far more completely than his father had, his own story, and the description of his children and the wife who had kept him from home.

On the way from Grenaa to Vejlby, walking beside the parson's white mare as his sister rode, Peder had learned from Anna all that the fishermen had been unable to tell him concerning the parson's case. He had no recollection of Judge Thorwaldsen. At the time of Peder's flight, Tryg had not yet assumed any importance in the county. He seemed a fine enough fellow; had not this trouble of his father's come up, he would have been a fortunate match for Anna. Yet in spite of Anna's assurances that Tryg Thorwaldsen would not let their father perish, from all she said of Tryg's integrity, it seemed plain to Peder that their greatest danger lay in Tryg's very honesty; and although he did not urge this opinion on his sister, he was worried.

Anna herself was in two minds, happy at Peder's return and at the change in her father's attitude, and sick at heart at her father's words about her marriage. Her face lightened and darkened, like a pool when clouds shift before the sun, transparent in her emotions. It had been a great comfort that night to know that her brother was sleeping in the parson's room, and it was a great comfort in the morning to see him riding ahead, beside Lars Sondergaard, toward Rosmos. Yet even such comfort could not dispel the double dread and sickness with which she thought of the approaching trial. She had not seen Tryg Thorwaldsen in three weeks. For three weeks she had longed hourly for him, and now she feared to see his face.

The town was crowded. The hearing had gained such notoriety that it was to be held in the inn, and the innyard was so crowded that the party from Vejlby hardly found accommodation for their mounts. As they pushed their way toward the inn door, a voice cried out, "There is the parson's daughter!" and all heads swung in their direction like leaves in a strong wind. Then other voices called to Anna, and many people blessed her and declared that all would be well because all the countryside knew of the goodness of Sören Qvist. Still all these people seemed strangers to her.

Close to the inn door, however, she recognized two men whom she would have avoided if she could, but the pressure of the crowd left her space only to pass within a half arm's length of them. One was Villum Ström and the other was Morten Bruus. It was customary for the accuser to pay the fee of the executioner, and there were at that time in prison in Copenhagen men who had lived for years behind locked doors and under sentence of death, to whom the executioner never came because the accuser had not found it convenient to provide the ten rix-dollars, or seven, or twelve, as the severity of the penalty might be. There had never been any doubt, in this case, of the accuser's willingness to pay the twelve rix-dollars provided for beheading with the sword, which was the parson's right, if he must die, rather than the disgrace of the gallows rope. But it was hardly a decent thing for Morten to be standing on this day so close to Villum Ström.

When she was almost upon him, unwillingly near, and so suddenly that she had no time to look the other way, Morten turned and bowed, as if surprised, with almost the same exaggerated courtesy and admiration with which he had saluted her in the parsonage kitchen when he had come to ask her hand in marriage. Intent upon her love and her fear, she had forgotten that he had once wished to marry her. She had thought of him only as the persecutor of her father. But she remembered now, with a shock, seeing the admiration in his eyes, his face being so close to hers that the glass-green of the iris was clear and the thick line of the black lashes. It frightened her that he should be smiling. She barely brushed Villum Ström with her glance, and pushed on after Peder Sörensen as fast as she was able, yet as she stepped across the threshold she could not help hearing Morten remark, in an overloud voice: "The saying has ever been, friend Villum, Martinmas is the best time for the killing of pigs."

The people from Vejlby parsonage were given space as near the judge's table as might be. There was a vacant bench reserved not far from them, but elsewhere every corner of the room was jammed, and Anna, before she bent her head above her hands to pray, as one does upon entering a church, saw that the windows were crowded with faces. The room was not quiet. The air was dense with expectation, and the hum of voices was dull and continuous, although now and then a single voice broke from the burden of hushed speech, and now and then a sudden laugh. Anna sat between Peder Sörensen and Vibeke. Just before her were Kirsten of the parsonage, with Hans, and Lars Sondergaard. She could see quite plainly, before the judge's table, the empty chair intended for the prisoner. But they were early; or there had been some delay. Neither the judge nor the prisoner appeared.

A man behind her drew a piece of bread from his pocket and a bit of bacon—she could smell it quite plainly although she did not turn her head—and began to munch. She heard him explain to his neighbor: "I had to be early to get in, I tell you. So I missed my breakfast. I could do with a can of beer."

The man beside him said, "Are you from Vejlby?"

"Not I," said the first speaker. "I come from Hallendrup. But who hasn't heard of the parson? I, for one, am for him. May he confound his enemies."

"In God's name," assented the other. "Yet it remains to be seen whether he is innocent. Yes, it looks to be a very interesting trial. And in another way."

"How so?" said the man from Hallendrup.

"Is not the judge the parson's son-in-law?" said the other.

"Something of the sort," said the man from Hallendrup, "or would have been, soon. Well, and I can see your point, friend. There is something in that."

Still the judge did not appear, nor the prisoner. Talk flagged a little as the people tired, and the heavy hum of voices ebbed, rose a little in one corner of the room, then in another, then faded away again. But the patience of the audience was great, as was the interest. The room grew close. When she had left the farm, the morning had been chill, the damp air clinging and penetrating, and Anna had wrapped herself in her warmest cloak. Now, though the room grew warm, she still held it close about her, as if it afforded her some needed privacy and protection. It was very hard to wait. Surely something must have happened to change the hour. Surely, three weeks ago, Tryg had said, at this same hour, and that had been much earlier. And as she struggled to put down the fear that the parson had become ill, the room fell suddenly dead quiet. A door was opening, beyond the magistrate's table. The prisoner entered the room.

The chain between his ankles dragged upon the boards as he went slowly forward to the chair reserved for him. He looked in good health, although he had grown thin. His face was perfectly serene, and he searched for only a moment in the crowd before he saw his children, and smiled at them. It was an unforced smile and lighted all his face.

"God be praised," said Anna to herself with a great rush of tenderness and relief, "God be praised and raise us up a witness."

Judge Thorwaldsen made his entry a few minutes later. Unlike the prisoner, the judge looked like a man who had been desperately ill. Gaunt and very tall in his black garments, his face, above the white ruff, looking bonier than ever, he moved forward to the table and seated himself behind it, glancing neither to the right nor to the left, nor searching through the crowd of onlookers for any special face. In the cold light his flaxen hair looked almost white, and all the blueness seemed to have ebbed from his eyes. Anna, at the sight of him, was shocked, first filled with pity, then with fear, since the grimness of his appearance seemed to forecast a dread decision. She wished him to look at her, then was afraid that he would, and turned her eyes away from him toward her father's tranquil countenance. The trial began.

It went forward very slowly, word after word remembered and foretold, like a bad dream in which one foreknows the end but still must slowly trace each tragic moment. The charge was made again, in the same words as on the former hearing, and the parson again denied it. The witnesses came forward one by one and made their depositions. Again the Widow Kirsten gave her evidence, and again her daughter Elsa told of laughing and talking with Niels by the hedge. He had given her nuts. He had said, "Wait and you shall hear a preachment." Again the laborer Jens Larsen told of returning by moonlight from Tolstrup, of taking off his wooden shoes and climbing the stile, of seeing the parson leveling the earth in his moonlit garden. Again Hans and Lars Sondergaard and Vibeke told of the exhumation of the corpse, and each affirmed, beyond any doubt, that he had recognized the miserable flesh as the body of his comrade Niels Bruus. Anna knew each sentence before it was spoken. She could not deny any of it, taken bit by bit, but of the whole picture she could not believe anything. For Peder Sörensen, although he had been told the substance of it, the presentation came as something new. He leaned forward, more and more sharply absorbed, and, without touching him, but hearing the light, changed rhythm of his breathing, knowing how quietly he sat, Anna was aware of the growing tension and excitement, violent under his outward calm. The maid Kirsten gave her story of seeing the parson in the passageway with the moonlight shining on his white cap and green dressing gown, and then, in a passion of regret which but made her sincerity beyond question, buried her head in Anna's lap and wept. Again each detail of the parson's long quarrel with Niels Bruus was brought forward, and every added speech fell upon Anna's heart like the drops of slow summer rain that gradually drag the heavy-headed blades of rye down to the sodden earth and hold them there. Judge Thorwaldsen listened with his head bent, leaning on his hand, and looked at no one, save when he summoned in turn each witness. He was as remote from the girl who sat and watched him as if he had never touched her hand.

When all the former witnesses had been called, the judge conferred a moment with the clerk. Then, looking about the room, he said: "The court delayed this case on the information that two new witnesses had offered to testify. Are those witnesses present?"

There was a slight commotion in the back of the room as two peasants stood up and tried to make their way forward. Everyone turned to look at them, the parson also, but Anna looked only at her father, and she saw in his face such expectation and hope that she was certain he looked now for a miracle. Such an expression of hope in so candid a face seemed to her then the final proof and statement of his innocence. But she was the only person in the room who saw it.

The two peasants gave their names, and were sworn to tell the truth. They were cousins, and from Tolstrup. The first one spoke for both of them.

"What we have to say is just the same. We were together—we both saw the same thing. It was on the night after the day when folks say Niels Bruus ran away from the parson."

Anna clasped and unclasped her hands, and she heard Peder draw a deep breath.

"We were coming home late from a dance. It was very late, but the moon was shining. We came along the road on the eastern side of Parson Sören's garden, and as we went we met a man coming from the direction of the woods along the road toward the garden. He was carrying a sack which looked very heavy. He was bent over with it, so that his face was shadowed and we could not see it. He was wearing a white nightcap—the moon shone very bright on it—and a long gown that I took to be of a green color. He passed us on the road and went on."

Chapter Seventeen

Thorwaldsen said, "You did not recognize this man, when you passed him, as the parson?"

But before the witness could answer, he was interrupted by a loud cry from the prisoner himself. Sören Qvist had risen to his feet. His face had become very pale, so that the tanned skin had the color of a winter leaf, surrounded by the frosty white of his hair and beard. His eyes had become exceedingly bright.

"I am ill," he cried, "very ill." Then he swayed, and before anyone could reach him he fell full length to the floor.

In the startled silence Morten Bruus leaped to his feet. "Ah ha!" he cried frantically. "That jogged the parson's memory!"

The room was immediately in an uproar. People rushed forward to the parson, and with difficulty, for he was still very heavy in spite of his thinness, lifted him and bore him from the room. Everyone was standing or moving. People surged between Anna and her father. She could barely see him as he was carried from the room. She stepped across the bench in front of her, holding up her long skirts, ran a few steps forward, stumbled over someone's foot, and almost fell. Half a dozen hands reached out to catch her. She pulled herself free from their aid and struggled forward still, past the judge's table, the prisoner's chair, pushing and shoving until she reached the door, which was closed. She stood there and beat upon it with her fists. She did not know or even wonder what had become of Peder or of Vibeke. She wanted only to reach her father.

215

The Trial of Sören Qvist

Suddenly the door opened, she was pulled through into the corridor, and the door was shut and barred behind her. The noise and uproar of the room was cut off abruptly, muted, like a mouth when a hand is clapped across it. She stood in a semi-darkness.

Chapter 18

The pastor regained consciousness very slowly. Those who were watching him saw him move his hand a little, then, after an interval, he opened his eyes, but he did not look at any of them. The eyes, focused as if upon some very remote object, might, in their rapt and steady concentration, have been observing an apocalyptic vision. His lips were still colorless, and his breathing light and irregular. Then the color began to return to the lips, a faint brushing in of pink upon a gray base, and the concentration of the eyes broke. The gaze wavered and looked upon the beamed ceiling, the walls and furnishings of the unfamiliar room. The skin became covered with a cold, heavy sweat. The parson turned his head and, perceiving Tryg Thorwaldsen standing near him, lifted one hand a little from the wrist and said faintly: "Anna. Where is Anna?"

The jailer broke in nervously, "Parson Sören, are you well again? In God's name, you gave us a scare."

The parson answered, still very softly, "I have a confession to make. Where is Anna?"

"She is waiting in the corridor, Parson Sören."

"I must have her by me," said the parson. He drew a deep breath, which he released very slowly. The color now seemed returning in normal measure to his face, and Thorwaldsen, taking a handkerchief from his pocket, wiped the sweat from the old man's forehead.

"I have a confession to make," repeated Sören Qvist. "Send for your clerk, that what I say may be taken down."

At a sign from Tryg the jailkeeper left the apartment, ushering out with him those who had helped to carry the parson from the public hall. The judge and the prisoner were left alone. Thorwaldsen drew up a chair beside the bench where the parson was lying and sat down beside his friend. Again he wiped the parson's face. He laid his own hand upon the parson's and, feeling how wet and cold was the parson's, tried to chafe it a little. The parson turned his head toward Tryg, without lifting it from the bench at all, and, looking very earnestly into Tryg's face, said, still in so faint a voice that the magistrate had to bend nearer to hear it: "The ways of God are past all understanding. He hath raised me up a witness, in answer to my prayer, and that witness is myself."

He said nothing more until the jailkeeper returned, bringing with him both Anna Sörensdaughter and the clerk of the court. Anna went straight to her father and, kneeling beside him, covered his hand with kisses. He dragged his free hand slowly across his body to touch her head, and they remained so, father and daughter, while the clerk set up his writing materials.

"I am ready now, Sir Judge," said the clerk.

"Are you ready? Then so am I," said the parson in a stronger voice. "Stay as you are, dear heart. This is a dreadful thing for you, but God will give you strength to bear it, as He will give to me, I trust. Oh, but it is a hard thing for me to say. I am guilty of the death of Niels Bruus.

"I could not imagine at first how it could have come to pass, but now I understand. Be patient with me, for I shall have to explain many things."

"But I am sure you never killed Niels Bruus," said Anna passionately, interrupting her father's quiet words. "You are ill, and you are deceiving yourself. Tryg, is it not so, that he talks so wildly because he is ill?"

She turned to Tryg then for the first time, but quite naturally, as if they had been together every day for the last three weeks, and as if there had never been a moment of doubt or hesitation in her mind. Tryg touched her very lightly on the shoulder.

"Wait," he said. "Let him speak."

"I am not deceived," said the parson. "I beg you to accept my confession and believe me."

"If I believe you, it is only because you ask me to," said the girl. "Peder, also, Peder will never believe you guilty, unless you bid him to."

"Peder?" said Sören Qvist with a look of bewilderment. "Is it my Peder that you talk of? But he has been gone these many years. We have believed him dead." His eyes met those of his daughter in question, then in startled remembrance. He could not speak, but his eyes

219

filled with tears which overran the lids and streamed down the side of his face into the thick white hair. Anna tried to wipe them away with the tips of her fingers.

"My mind is indeed infirm," he said at length. "I am like one struck by the lightning of God. I am dazed, and stupid, but I have seen a thing very clearly. Such a thing as could make me forget even my Peder. Now I shall tell you." He looked beyond Anna to the 'clerk, and, as if at a signal, that man dipped his quill in the ink. The parson began:

"From my childhood, as far back as I can remember, I have been passionate and quarrelsome, impatient of contradiction, and ever ready with a blow. Yet I have seldom let the sun go down upon my wrath, nor have I borne ill will to anyone. If I have been quick to anger, I have also been prompt in forgiveness. You all know that.

"Once, when I was but a little boy, I killed a dog that stole my dinner. Again, when I was a student in Leipsic, I quarreled with a German youth. I challenged him, and in the duel I wounded him severely, yet, praise God, I did not kill him. But it was God who spared his life, not I, and now I feel that the punishment is come upon me for that I wished to kill him. Now that I am old and a father, now that I might be happy with a son and a daughter, it falls with tenfold weight! Ah, Father in Heaven, it is here that the wound is the sorest."

At this point he began to weep again, and it was only after a long pause that he was able to continue.

Chapter Eighteen

"I will now confess the crime which I have no doubt committed, but of which I am still, nevertheless, not fully conscious. That I struck Niels with my spade, I know full well. I thought that I struck with the flat of the spade and that I did him little harm. He fell down at my feet, and I surely assisted him to rise. Then he broke from my arms and ran away. All this I know surely. What followed—heaven help me!—four witnesses have seen, yet I remember nothing of it: namely, that I fetched the corpse from the wood and buried it in the garden. I will now tell you why I am constrained to believe that this is true.

"Three or four times in my life, that I know of, it has happened to me to walk in my sleep. The last time, which was about nine years ago, I was the next day to preach a funeral sermon over the remains of a man who had unexpectedly met with a dreadful death. I was at a loss for a text, when the words of a wise man among the ancient Greeks suddenly occurred to me, 'Call no man happy until he be in his grave.' To use the words of a heathen text for a Christian discourse was not, as I thought, seemly; but then I remembered that the same thought expressed in well nigh the same terms was to be met with somewhere in the Apocrypha. I sought and sought, but could not find the passage. It was late; I was wearied with much previous labor. I therefore went to bed and fell sound asleep.

"Greatly did I marvel the next morning when, on arising and seating myself at my writing desk, I saw before me written in large letters on a piece of paper,

'Let no man be deemed happy before his end cometh. Sirach, xi: 34.' But not this alone. I found likewise a funeral discourse, short, but as well written as any I had ever composed, and all in my own handwriting. In the chamber none other than I could have been. I knew, therefore, who it was that had written the discourse, and that it was no other than myself.

"Not more than half a year previous I had, in the same marvelous state, gone in the night into the church and fetched away a handkerchief which I had left in the chair behind the altar. Mark now.

"When the two witnesses this morning delivered their evidence before the court, then my previous sleep-walkings suddenly flashed before me; and I also recalled that in the morning after that dreadful night I had been surprised to see my dressing gown lying on the floor just inside the door, whereas it has always been my custom to hang it on a chair near my bed-side. Niels, unhappy Niels, must have fallen down dead in the wood. I must in my sleepwalking have followed him thither. Yes, the Lord have mercy! So it was. So it must have been."

The scratching of a pen upon paper followed the last words, so loud in the silence that it was like an echo. "So it must have been."

The scribe laid down his quill with a half-furtive look at the three others of the pastor's audience, who sat as still as if they had all been touched themselves by the lightning of God of which the pastor had spoken, or as if they gazed upon a strange landscape lightened unbearably. The pastor was the first to speak. He addressed the judge.

"So, my dear friend, if you would be kind to me, you will pronounce my sentence as speedily as possible, and you will also arrange that the punishment be exacted with the least possible delay."

Anna cried out then, "No, no, Tryg! You cannot do that!"

Tryg, turning to her, his face as white and strained as her own, said gently, "But if I do not, then another will."

And the pastor, whose voice was quite clear and steady now, raising himself upon one elbow, said, "He is right, dear child. Let my story be finished by a friend, rather than by a stranger." He smiled a little. "You were never willing to have an old horse sold to the tallow man, that it should die among strangers."

"But it is not just," said Anna to Tryg, "that a man should suffer punishment for a deed unconsciously committed."

But her father answered, with a gesture of the opened hand, "Waking or sleeping, I am responsible for whatever I have done." Then his composure began to waver. He looked from his daughter to the judge, then said to Thorwaldsen, speaking with great difficulty, "I commend her to you. Care for her." Then he lay down again and turned his face toward the wall.

As Anna rose to her feet, the three men also stood up. Tryg spoke to the jailer, instructing him to escort Anna to her brother. He turned then to Anna. The girl stood drawing her cloak tightly about her and looked up at him as if she were going to speak, her eyes searching his face to question and reproach.

At the first shock of the parson's confession, Tryg had felt a great surge of relief. The burden of decision had been removed from him. He had not realized how hard the strain of indecision and responsibility had been until it was unexpectedly withdrawn. He felt like a man released from the rack. This first reaction lasted only a moment, barely long enough for him to realize it and be humiliated by it. A natural grief and affection followed swiftly upon it, drawing him close, closer than ever, to the parson and to Anna. It was a good and noble emotion and would have eased his heart like an outpouring of tears save that it could not quite blot out that fleeting sense of guilt. The face before him was so young that in spite of the fatigue and sorrow of the last weeks it kept a freshness, a snowy transparency; it made him think again of the first wild flowers of the beechwoods, that were more akin in substance to the snow which they replaced than to the verdure to follow them. The eyes too were spring-like in their clearness and coolness, the first pale golden sunlight in the woods. Under their light scrutiny Tryg felt his tenderness increase, and his trouble; and Anna read in his affection a confusion which she did not understand.

"If you love me," he said, "you will go home now, and wait for me there." He put out his hands toward her, but she stepped backward quickly, so that his fingers barely brushed the wool of her garment. He let his hands drop in an expression of despair. She did not know why she had avoided him; the moment she realized what she had done, she was sorry. But the instinctive gesture could not well be apologized for, nor explained away. She stood a moment, wishing with all her heart that she might apologize, but they were not alone. She turned to the jailkeeper, and together they left the room.

In the corridor they passed a guard and went onward, their steps echoing between bare walls. At the door of the courtroom they paused, and before the jailer unbarred it he said awkwardly: "It is a pity, mistress, as you say, and not just, that so good a man must suffer for something that he never knew he did; no, nor ever meant to do. Also, we shall miss you when you do not come any more to visit us. But God's will be done."

The words of kindness, when she had least expected any, and from a man from whom she had expected nothing, touched her deeply, so much so that when they reached Peder and Vibeke, and Peder inquired of Anna, "Who is this man?" Anna could only think to answer, "He is a man who has been very kind to me."

Peder looked after the jailkeeper, who had already moved away into the crowd, and frowned slightly. Then his brow cleared. "But of course," he said. "I remember him now."

Then Anna told her story, simply and briefly. It did not become more real in the telling. She saw the incredulous horror grow in Vibeke's eyes, saw the face of Peder darken, and from the depth of her own despair hardly felt for their distress. When she had finished, Vibeke said, "He is clean out of his mind."

"It is what he believes," said Anna. "He bids us to believe it too."

Vibeke shut her soft lips firmly and shook her head. Peder said only: "Vibeke, see that she reaches Vejlby safely. I will join you there later."

Chapter 19

That afternoon the wind began to blow a little, shifting the mist that had overhung the countryside. As Anna and her companions left Rosmos, riding on slowly past wooded knolls and gently rolling farmland, lights and shadows began to change above the trees; the oaks shone suddenly coppery bright as a patch of sunlight moved across them. The field beyond was a sudden emerald, with sprouting aftermath; and there were distances of deep, aqueous blue. But the sunlight was intermittent, and when the sun was clouded again, the oaks shone dull like copper pans through the peat smoke of a shadowy kitchen.

Anna, riding her father's big white mare, Vibeke going ahead, the other servants following, listened to the hoofbeats on the hard earth and was aware of the worn leather of the reins between her fingers, of the crisp coarse hair of the mane blowing back along the mare's neck. She watched the light change on tree and field, and noticed with an unexpected happiness a bit of clear blue shining against the dark edge of a cloud.

She was aware of these things with a clear immediate perception, but beyond them her mind seemed clouded, and dimmer than the sky, and she rode as in a waking dream. Vibeke had taken charge of affairs. She left everything to Vibeke.

At Aalsö they paused, and Vibeke sent the others on to Vejlby. Anna she detained, with a hand on the white mare's bridle. The girl did not wonder or protest as they turned toward the Aalsö parsonage. The hoofbeats sounded hollow upon the wooden bridge before the house of Peder Korf. The stream below was running full and clear. Anna looked down as they crossed it, and thought she saw below the silver current, the bending tufts of cresses. She dismounted without aid and stood waiting, the reins in her hand, for the parson's boy to take charge of the horses, and while she waited she observed with a gentle pleasure, as she had observed the changing colors under the moving clouds, how the beech leaves, pale golden lozenges, floated down through the damp air and lay upon the earth thick as stars in a dim summer sky. Her pleasure was quite impersonal and removed from the sense of her own tragedy. She marveled that she should be at once so sorrowful and yet so conscious of the beauty of the day. She seemed to have arrived at a great pause in her existence. Her father had accused himself, and Tryg had accepted the accusation. All the hope and trust by which she had lived since the hour of her father's arrest had been cut away abruptly. She had no plan now. She did not know what to do next.

Chapter Nineteen

The beech leaves continued to fall with every little gust of wind. The new thatch of the roof gleamed softly with a golden sheen. The front wall of the parsonage had no windows, but the thatch drew down warmly about the doorway, and the door was wide. About the doorstone the grass was worn away, a sign of hospitality. A little beyond the door, the wall jogged forward where the New Room had been built, and all was freshly whitewashed. The air smelled of autumn, a compounded fragrance sweet to breathe, and she heard the steady gurgle of the stream. The white mare turned her head, and the girl felt on the hand that held the reins the warm breath of inquiring nostrils. When the horses had been led away, she followed Vibeke into the kitchen, and thence into the New Room, where Peder Korf received them.

He had not been at the trial. He had only a short time before returned from an errand in the parish, and had heard nothing of Sören Qvist's confession. Anna let Vibeke tell the story, and let Vibeke meet the outpouring of Peder Korf's astonishment and sympathy. She noted, as if it were fated, how simply he accepted the self-accusation. She thought that, like Tryg, he was strangely content with it. She could not yet accept it herself. Yet he had been as hopeful yesterday as herself.

"So good a man," he murmured. "He had but one fault, and that it should have overcome him in this fashion! So good a man. And my friend."

She heard him promise to attend her father for the last communion, heard Vibeke thank him, heard herself thank him, and turned away, thinking the errand done. But Vibeke hung back. She had yet a kindness to ask of Peder Korf.

"When a man dies," said Vibeke, "all is not finished. There is yet a burying. And when a man is beheaded as a criminal, he is not allowed to lie in holy ground. Yet surely Parson Sören should be buried in a churchyard. If Niels Bruus, who made nothing but trouble in all his life, and in his death, too, shall lie buried in holy ground, how can we bear the thought that a man as kind as Sören Qvist should sleep forever under stones and nettles? Forgive me, Parson Peder, if I speak out of turn. No, do not look at me with such a shocked face. Indeed, I am at my wit's end now. I do not mean to be without respect."

Peder Korf answered, "I do not mean to be shocked. It is only that I had not thought ahead to the burying. You are right. It is a bitter thing that one of God's shepherds should be denied the right to sleep in holy ground. Still, it is not meet that a criminal be buried in the churchyard."

Anna said not a word, but Vibeke protested stoutly, "Parson Sören was never a criminal."

"He will die the death of a criminal," said Peder Korf.

"Ah, Pastor Peder," cried Vibeke, "you know right well that left to yourself you would never deny him holy burial. Who is there in this parish or the next would blame you for putting him to rest where he should rightly lie? Only Morten Bruus, perhaps, who is a devil."

"I think," said Peder Korf, passing a hand over his brow in some bewilderment, "that Morten Bruus is little concerned with anything beyond the fortunes of this world."

"Then," said Vibeke, pressing her point, "you may bury him in Aalsö churchyard, and none to inquire."

So Peder Korf assented, as much in answer to Anna's silence as to Vibeke's pleading. "We will bury him after dark," he said, "and none shall know who need not."

He gave them his blessing then, and they departed. Returned at last to Vejlby, Anna still moved under Vibeke's direction. In her waking dream she prepared for a last visit to her father. Vibeke set out bread and meat.

"He will not be hungry," said Anna.

"He is still alive," said the housekeeper sharply. "He must eat."

She brought out his black robe and white gauffered collar and freshened the delicate fluting.

"He must be fitly clothed on the morrow," said Vibeke.

And from the chest she drew the linen sheet which had been woven for the wedding bed.

"He must be shrouded," said Vibeke. "We cannot let him die like a beggar."

Anna was sitting in the Bride's Room with the smooth linen spread upon her knees when Peder Qvist returned. It smelled of the summer's lavender and was as soft and heavy as cream. She stroked it gently and smiled a little, remembering the happiness with which

231

she had woven it, and finding the texture still even and rich. The smile was still in her eyes as she lifted them to her brother's face, and she continued to smile, at seeing him again. To Peder she seemed like a child unaware of the troubles of his elders. He closed the door and crossed the room rapidly, knelt by her side and said with great gentleness, as to a child, "This is all well done, but, God willing, we shall not need that fine shroud."

To his great relief, the smile faded from her eyes, her color quickened; she woke from her strange dream and said, in a whisper, but clearly and with vigor, "Peder, you will not let him die?"

"I did not come from Skaane just to receive his blessing," said her brother. "The plan is this. You will go this evening to the jail with food, and with the other things you have prepared. There will be no one in the outer room when it is time for you to leave. The doors will be unlocked. You will bring him the short way to the river. The streets are dark, and there will be friends on guard. There will be a boat—my friends from Skaane—ready to leave for Varberg. You must be warmly clothed. And in a few days at the longest we will all be in a new home, and you will find a sister, and our father another daughter."

"But," she said, "will we not be followed?"

"We will be out of Denmark, and beyond Danish law," he said. "And who knows where I live, save Vibeke, who will never tell?" He had talked with the jailkeeper, who had met him more than halfway with his plan. The men from Skaane had been glad to help, as well. The jailer had undertaken to have the streets watched, lest some unfriendly person find the jail unguarded.

"You have heard, have you not," he said, "that sentence has been passed, and the execution set for tomorrow morning? Therefore we have only this evening, and we must be prompt."

"Tryg pronounced the sentence?" she said. And then, "But he had no choice. Our father bade him do so. Oh, Peder, I wish that I might see Tryg once more. I was unkind to him when I left him. Do you not think that he might come with us? We could all be so happy together. Do you not think I might ask him?"

Her brother hesitated. Then he said, "And if he did not come with us?"

"There would be no harm done, would there?"

"He would be obliged to prevent us."

"Oh, I do not think he would!" she cried. But even as she spoke the image of Tryg's face appeared to her as she had last seen it, with the uncomprehended trouble in the eyes, and she remembered her father's warning.

"If you are quite sure that he will come with us, then ask him," said Peder gently. "But if you doubt at all, then you must not risk his knowing. It is too great a burden to put upon his honor."

"I would go with him, if he were running away," she said, "no matter what he might have done, nor to what strange land he were going." She looked down at the soft linen on her knees, and hardly saw it, because of the sickness in her heart. "Oh, my love, my

233

love," she thought. Then she said aloud, "I will not ask him."

It was hard to leave Vibeke, but she needed no excuse for her tears. Every day since the imprisonment of Sören Qvist, when Anna had ridden to Grenaa to visit him, Vibeke had accompanied her and waited for her. Tonight Peder Qvist would ride with her, but the housekeeper grieved to let her go. Again she offered to ride with them.

"There is no need for you to tire yourself, Vibeke," said Peder Qvist. "Tomorrow will be a hard day, and you will have much to do." Then, to the housekeeper's surprise, he leaned from his horse and kissed her, first on one cheek, then on the other, so that the tears sprang to her eyes, and she turned away, her apron over her face, and did not see them, the brother and sister who had been her children, as they rode away under the trees.

Before Anna on her saddle rested a willow basket containing food, the black ornat and the fluted ruff. Under her cape she carried on her arm a bag containing a few personal belongings. Strangely enough, she was no longer tired.

A few stars were coming out, and the air had not yet lost its blueness. The wind was becoming less fitful, although not strong, and the clouds were clearing from the sky. They rode on between copse and field without speaking until they drew near to Aalsö common. Here was a knoll called Raven's Hill, which had been used for years for the sad business of public punishment. As the two riders came within sight of it, Anna could observe a few men busy with beams and boards. They were building not a scaffold, but a platform. Peder turned to her then and said, "Never fear," and they rode on, beyond sight of the meadow.

It was dark when they reached the innyard at Grenaa, where they left their horses. They went on foot to the jail. Those few persons whom they passed on the way looked at them curiously, knowing who they were, but none ventured to address them. All this was not outside of Peder's plan. At the jail door they halted, in the darkness.

"You are sure you will not be afraid?" he asked. "It is better if three of us are not seen together. You will have him draw his cloak about his face, and if you are met, he may pass for your brother. We will wait for you until midnight, but come as soon as you can."

"I am not afraid," she answered.

"And you are sure of the way?"

"Yes, I am sure," she said. "I remember everything that you have told me."

"I am sorry I have to leave you," he said.

Chapter 20

The jail wife was seated near the fire with her child in her arms. She looked up briefly as Anna entered the room, but did not greet her. The jailkeeper came from a shadowy corner and went directly to the door to the inner room, which he unlocked and held open. Nor did he speak to Anna, and the girl, remembering his friendliness of the morning, found it strange. The basket cumbersome in one hand, the weight of her small parcel of belongings tugging at the arm beneath the cape, she made her way awkwardly past the jailkeeper to the inner room and jostled him unintentionally with her basket in so doing.

"Pardon me," she exclaimed softly, and though he nodded, he did not open his lips, and he turned away from her promptly.

However, as the door was drawn closed behind her, although she listened carefully, she did not hear the final click of the latch.

She stood a moment, looking across the dimly lighted inner room. There seemed to be no one in any of the corners, though a pile of fresh straw lay tumbled under the high small window. Her father lay on the bed, and a candle was burning, set in a ring in the wall near by him. It was a tallow candle. It smoked, and smelled of grease. She saw her father's eyes turn toward her as she entered. He did not move else.

He was not manacled. As if his keepers thought him too weak and broken to be able to move, he had been permitted to lie down like any dying man upon the hard wooden bed. As Anna approached him, he lifted both hands, and when she had set the basket down and knelt beside him, he took her face in his hands and looked at her long and lovingly before he kissed her.

"Well," he said, "in God's kindness I shall soon be free, and my child will not need to come any more to this place of sorrow."

"Oh yes," she said eagerly, "you will soon be free Are you strong? I have brought you meat and wine. Could you walk a little distance, after you have eaten? Only a little distance?"

"Why, that is thoughtful of you," said her father, "but I am not hungry. And I can walk as far as I shall need to. God will give me strength."

"No, no, not that," she said quickly, and glanced over her shoulder at the door to make sure that they were still alone. "Peder has talked to friends. We are to go away together, tonight. We are to go with Peder to Skaane, where all will be safe and we can be together."

Her father looked at her in bewilderment, and she hurried to explain the steps that Peder had taken, the sympathy of the jailkeeper, the friendliness of the fishermen from Skaane. "And so," she finished, "we shall be upon the ocean tonight, with only the free air about us and the free water under the boat."

"Peder has planned all this?" said the old man in a tone of wonderment. "What a good son! Truly, I am blessed in my children. You must thank him for me, little Anna, and tell him that he has made me happy."

"You can thank him yourself," said Anna. "And we will all be happy. You will have grandchildren to climb on your knees, and the fields and the woods of Skaane —are they not as fair as those of Jutland?"

"Peder's children," said the old man, smiling. "What a joy to see them! Do you think, little Anna, that they look like Peder?"

"Surely, surely," said Anna. "And they will love you. Take a little bread, Father, and see if you can rise without being dizzy. For we must go quickly."

But the old man shook his head. "It is a happy dream," he said, "but I cannot go." Nevertheless he continued to smile at her, his whole face illuminated and content. After a while he said softly, "Praise be to God, I do not wish to go."

Anna cried out, "Oh, do not say so! You are not so weak. It is but a little way to walk, and you shall put your arm on my shoulder and lean on me, and when you are free, you will feel well again."

"No, no," said the old man. "You do not understand. I am happy to stay. Your wish for me has made me happy, but I am happier still in that I do not wish to go."

Chapter Twenty

"If you would but make a little effort," pleaded the girl.

"I thank God that He moves me to stay and meet my fate," said her father in a new tone of firmness and finality.

"Then you will not come?" she said, realizing less the meaning of the words than the tone of the voice, and her face grew very sad. "Oh, do not ask me to leave you here."

Her father spoke more gently, with a great tenderness. "You know better than anyone," he said, "you who have come to me so kindly every day in this foul place, you know how I have suffered. Not the weight of the chains, not the fear of death, but the thought that my God had dealt with me unjustly so filled my soul with bitterness that I can never repent deeply enough. In my heart I reproached my Saviour that I should be regarded as a murderer. Yet I locked the innermost doors of my spirit upon the consciousness of mine iniquity. Rather than acknowledge my sin, I blamed my God for His unkindness to me, and for His unjustness. Did I not know all the time that He who is All Goodness could never be unjust?"

"You speak as if you were happy," said Anna, her eyes filling with tears.

"Truly, I believe I am happy," said the old man, again with wonder in his voice.

"Then you must feel yourself forgiven. Surely you have suffered enough, and repented enough. Why must you stay to suffer an earthly punishment, when you are forgiven in heaven?"

"I do not know whether I am forgiven or not," he said. "But if I should not stay, I remove myself from God's plan for me, and that I cannot do."

"God forgive," the girl cried, "it does not seem to me like God's plan, but that of the devil. It is a tangle and a trap. Did you not tell me so once yourself?" She sprang to her feet and, striking her hands together, paced a few steps away from him, and returned as quickly, as if in action she might find them some escape from the tangle.

But her father said, "Did I not say to you also, even the demons are servants of our Lord?"

"But Morten Bruus——" she began.

He interrupted her gently. "Even Morten Bruus is included in God's plan." The faintest shadow of a smile crossed his lips. "But what is Morten Bruus? At the most, an appearance of the devil. At the least a man who desired what he was not worthy to possess. Tonight he is of no consequence."

Anna stood looking down at her father, the light from the candle gilding the flesh of his hands and face, making his hair and beard shine white as salt. She saw nothing else in the room, not the stained floor, nor the chains, nor the coldly sweating stones. His quiet voice continued: "Tonight even the killing of Niels Bruus is of small consequence, or that I must die for it. Oh, it is not that I do not suffer to have slain him. But that sin was less than the sin that followed after, to have cried out with bitterness against my God. Forgiven or unforgiven, I know not how it is, but I feel my Lord so near me that my heart is filled with peace. It is like the most gentle light of evening upon the young fields of grain."

His voice died away in a whisper, and then there was no sound in the room save that of a girl weeping upon her father's breast.

The motion of the boat was acquiescent to the motion of the wave that sank behind the stern with a prolonged liquid gurgle, both boat and wave running before the light, steady wind. The prow made a soft crushing noise that swelled and faded in a long, slow rhythm. The sail held steady. Seated in the stern, with her cloak drawn close about her against the chill air from the water, Anna Sörensdaughter swayed to the easy motion of the boat. The world was darkness, lighted below from the pallor of the water reflected from the pallor of the sky. She could make out very dimly the shape of the sail, the shapes of men bent beneath the sail. A voice beside her said, with a strong Swedish accent, "Where the river goes into the sea there are fisherfolk dwelling. Poor houses, but I have known the people for a long time. They will have fire and a roof for us. You are not afraid?"

She answered that she was not afraid, and the voice commended her.

"He will not come," she had said to Peder. He had

helped her into the boat. Hands had reached up from the darkness and lifted her down to the place in which she was now sitting. There had been voices in a muffled conference, and the boat had been pushed free of the wharf. "Are you not coming?" she had called to Peder, in a sudden panic, but he had answered, "I go to Raven's Hill in the morning. I will meet you. You are with friends." And the last words had come small and fading across the widening stretch of water; yet she had believed him, and her fear had gone. It was strange, nevertheless, that she should not feel afraid. The voices which spoke to her were kindly, although the accent was foreign. She could not make out the features of a single countenance; and she had never been in a boat before. The floating motion of the boat, the balanced unsteadiness, were new to her, and yet familiar, as if she had experienced them before in a dream.

Obedient, unreconciled, alone, she had crossed the empty outer room of the jail, had let herself out, and, still alone, had traversed the dark streets of Grenaa till she came to the water front. Somewhere along the way the thought had come to her that there was now no reason for flight. She could return to Vejlby. She could even return to Tryg. Her father had commended her to Tryg's care. Yet even as it came the thought dissolved. There was no return. She had let herself be lifted into the boat, and the boat and the darkness had become all that was left of her world. Even Peder was gone.

"There are always those who would be glad to make

trouble for men from Skaane," said the voice beside her, above the soft noise of the water. "It is better to be away from the town."

Over heath and marsh the wind blew unobstructed from the southwest. The river widened; the shore on their right hand became so low and dark that it seemed but a shadow joining the water and the sky. There was no way in which to reckon the time, nor the distance which they covered, but by and by a new noise made itself heard above the wash of water running with the boat: the slow boom of the surf repeated with a rhythm far more slow than that of human breathing, just as inevitable as that of living breath. The open water of the Kattegat was before them, and beyond that water the realm of Skaane.

The sail dropped down. With poles and oars the boat was turned and brought to the northern shore, and beached there. Anna, guided by hands in the darkness, crept forward, past the swinging canvas to the prow, and from the peak was lifted down to a sandy beach swept by the wind and by thin running waves.

She went forward with the men from Skaane across the firm wet sand to the loose sand above the reach of the waves, where it was difficult to walk. Close to the dunes was a cluster of huts. The fishermen pounded on the door of the first hut, calling in Swedish peremptory and reassuring phrases, until the door was opened, and they all crowded within.

Never in her life had Anna considered such a dwelling, so small, so limited to the bare essential use of holding back the wind, the rain, the driven sand. Con-

structed of rubble and driftwood, old beams from lost
ships, plastered with clay upon wattles, the room had
no chimney, no window, and only the one door. The
floor was drifted with sand, and in the center of it
stood an iron brazier in which a few turfs smoked and
burned. The smoke curled up through the low rafters
and found its way out gradually through chinks under
the eaves, or sank in gray coils toward the floor. The
opening of the door made the turf blaze and glow for
an instant.

She stood among the fishermen from Skaane while
the spokesman for them explained to the dwellers in
the hovel that they were in need of shelter for a friend,
that they must wait here until morning for another
friend. For themselves, they would sleep in the boat,
but they had no place there for Anna. The man and
woman whose rest they had interrupted accepted the
charge without hesitation.

There was no light except from the smoldering peat,
but in its glow Anna had the first sight of the men who
had become her guardians until the return of her
brother. They shook hands with her, one after the
other, as they bade her good night and slipped out into
the wind, and she had an impression of many pale blue
eyes in reddened faces, of red wool caps and blue caps,
of strong and roughened hands, some cold to the touch
and some as warm as cakes. Then she was alone with
the man and woman of the dwelling.

The man was small and shrunken; his gray hair fell
down upon the red scarf wrapped round and round his
neck. He had risen from bed apparently just as he had

lain down to it, clothed fully, save for his shoes. His feet were bare. His wife, too, in her petticoat and shawl, was barefooted, but wore a torn blue kerchief spread over her hair and knotted under her chin. She was of a sturdier build than her husband, and probably some years younger. There was something familiar about her for Anna. Both were embarrassed and kind. They bade her sit down on a stool by the fire. They begged her to excuse them that they had no other room, no other bed, and, saddest of all, no other bed coverings.

"My man shall lie by the wall, I next, and you, mistress, where you can at least see the fire, although there is but little warmth in that. It is warmer to be three in a bed than all alone."

"You are very kind," said the girl.

"I do not ask what you are doing here," said the woman, "but you may be sure I wish you were in a better place. This is no fit place for Anna Sörensdaughter."

"I did not think they told you my name," said Anna.

"Mistress," said the woman, "it is not likely you would remember the fishwife from ten years back, but it is easy for me to remember the little girl who ran in and out of the kitchen."

"Then," said Anna, "you do not need to ask why I am here, with fishermen from Skaane. We wait for my brother Peder. You will believe that we cannot be gone from Denmark while my father is yet alive."

The woman gave a slight shrug. "Here is neither

Denmark nor Skaane," she said. "Here it is the end of the world. But you are among friends. Come and lie down, and if you keep your cloak about you, you will sleep the warmer."

For a long time after the fishwife and her man were sound asleep, Anna Sörensdaughter lay awake. The air was very close with the turf smoke and the smell of dried fish, yet she did not resent it. The very closeness was an added shelter against the wideness of the night from which she had come, the wideness of the ocean which lay before her on the morrow. She watched the antics of the smoke wreaths, following the flaws of the air. She heard the wind shake the hut and whip sand against it, and she heard the heavy breathing of those who had taken her into their own bed, humble as it was. The simplicity with which they had accepted her filled her with wonder, and yet it was of a piece with all that had befallen her that night. It was the simplicity of poverty and misfortune, which leave the issue clear. She thought of her father as she had last seen him, the white hair shining under the faint light of the tallow dip, the eyes, dark with distance, following her as she left the inner room. She thought of Vibeke, whose affection for her seemed like a flowering meadow across this night, and of creatures from the parsonage farm, the three-colored cat, the brown dog, and Golden Star, the daughter of Golden Rose, lying in the hay while she held the light for her father, and the parson of Vejlby kneeling with pride beside the newborn. Drowsiness crept upon her as her thoughts became only images and shifted without reason, until at last, in a trust which resembled the trust with which her father surrendered himself to his fate, his child surrendered herself to sleep. She hardly knew how great an act of faith she had performed.

Chapter 22

The girl slept long, the youthfulness of her body taking mastery over the sorrow of her mind. She slept deeply, below any dreaming remembrance of her grief, and when she woke she was refreshed and strengthened. Before she had opened her eyes she thought that she was in her own room at Vejlby. Then the lids fluttered open, and she saw, close above her head, the gray, waterworn timbers of the roof. She turned her head and saw the iron brazier standing three-legged on the sandy floor, and beyond it, against the wall, a stool, a chest, a twig broom leaning beside the door. The hovel was full of a cold gray light that seemed to have ebbed in through the gaps under the eaves. There was no one beside her on the bed, no one at all in the place, and, as she listened, she heard no voices without.

Terror seized her lest she should have been forsaken, lest the fishermen should have sailed without her, without Peder, lest Peder should not return. She pushed back the heavy, dirty covers with both hands and sat up, swinging her feet to the floor. And as she sat there, looking about in the dim light for her shoes, she heard the first voice, far down toward the river, and then another, not so distant, answering it, and the words were Swedish, she was sure of that. Relieved, she paused before she bent to pick up her shoes, and looked again about the small room which had given her hospitality.

The events of the day before returned to her mind in orderly detail. Yesterday she had been tossed from hope to despair, from hope again to a sense of loss which embraced everything which she had loved most in her young life, and she had lain down exhausted. Now she felt very calm and strong, and capable of meeting whatever the day might bring. The calmness was kindred to exaltation, although she did not think of it as such. This was the day for which she had made great preparations in her spirit. It could not take her unawares, like an unready housewife with the coming of great company.

She slipped her bare feet into the cold wooden shoes and made a few steps on the gritty floor toward the brazier, in which the fire seemed to have died. The door opened then, letting in a vast flood of gray light from the beach and the sea. The fishwife, entering, left the door open behind her. She must have been waiting just outside, to have picked up so quickly the first stirrings within. The girl saw then that the day, though sunless, was well advanced. The sky was thinly clouded over, and the sea the color of lead. As the long waves came in, the wind from the shore caught the breaking foam and blew it backward over their shoulders.

The fishwife approached Anna with solicitude, and, being assured that the girl had slept well, put more turfs on the fire and blew the smothered embers, shut the door, brought forth a basin of cold water, and helped the girl with her toilet. She lamented that she had no milk, only a thin fish soup and a little rye bread, but she set the soup to warm over the fire, and assured Anna that it was nourishing. She reverted to her memories of Anna in the parsonage kitchen, and added that she had seen her also on the streets of Grenaa. She went to Grenaa sometimes, she said, but no oftener than she had to, and Anna gathered that she had in some way become an outcast, that the people from the beach hovels hardly belonged in the same world with the townfolk or with farmers. This side of the river was beyond her father's parish, she knew, but it seemed, as the woman talked, to be outside of all parishes.

She was not at all clean, not at all like Vibeke, yet when she brought the bowl of hardly warm soup to the girl, and stood watching her take the first mouthfuls, there was something of Vibeke in her countenance. Beyond Anna's expectation, the soup, in spite of being not at all hot, was of a good flavor, and when she expressed her approval, the fishwife nodded her head and smiled. She had been waiting for that.

Peder Qvist returned to the inn at Grenaa, where he found the two horses, and left Grenaa, riding the brown horse and leading his father's white mare. He was unwilling to remain at the inn or anywhere in the outskirts of the town. Full of bitterness at his father's situation, and of resentment at having to return upon his plans, with no other plan clear in his mind, he took from force of habit the Vejlby road, and midnight found him at the village. He was unwilling to be seen. He had planned so carefully to disappear with Anna and his father that he still felt the compulsion to avoid being noticed. He could not return to the parsonage without incurring Vibeke's interrogations, and to seek shelter at the inn also meant talking with people who knew him, and they would wonder why he was not at the farm. The night was increasingly cold and he was tired; still, he passed by the inn, and presently found himself near to the parsonage, even as near as the outer fields. He dismounted here and sent both the horses into the field, thinking that he might be less noticeable on foot.

He had yet to spend the remainder of the night somewhere, and he thought of Peder Korf, and so took his way toward Aalsö. But when he came within a half mile of the parsonage it occurred to him that the Aalsö parson would question him regarding Anna. He might, besides, attempt to reconcile him to his father's fate, and Peder did not wish to be reconciled. So he passed by the entrance to the Aalsö parsonage and went on until he stood before the Inn of the Golden Lion. The coldness of the night, combined with the thought that no one here might know him, impelled him to push the door a little. The room was lighted warmly by the thick coals of what had been a good fire, and the innkeeper was a stranger to him. He spent the ebbing hours of the night here on a settle before the fire, and left early in the morning before anyone was stirring.

The Aalsö common, with the knoll called Raven's Hill, where the platform had been erected for the execution, was so easily reached that he found himself the first there, and felt compelled to go away again for fear he should be noticed. When the lanes began to fill with people, some on foot, some on horseback, and the common itself began to look as if a fair were to be held there, Peder gave up his aimless wanderings through the oak woods, the hedged lanes, and stationed himself at the edge of the open space, from which he could see well enough and still have close to him the shelter of the trees.

He had not been prepared for the quantity of people who would come to this spectacle. The meadow kept filling with little groups that clotted into larger groups. Under the veiled sky the colors of all the garments seemed very bright—scarlet shawls and blue skirts and russet coats and green or scarlet caps—and he realized as he watched that all these people had put on their holiday attire. There was talking, there was even occasional laughter, the sound rising suddenly and broken off quickly. But in the main they were quiet and they were very patient. They waited until almost noon before the two soldiers appeared upon the platform, followed by Villum Ström. After that it was only a few minutes before Sören Qvist appeared, followed by Parson Peder Korf. Then the crowd was very quiet.

The Trial of Sören Qvist

Peder Qvist saw that his father was clothed in the black robe and the white ruff of his calling. He saw him speak a few words with those beside him on the platform, as if making a request, which seemed to be granted. He then turned toward the crowd, which watched him with such great attention that they could not have missed his slightest gesture, and, folding his hands before him just as he did when he preached in the Vejlby church, just as Peder remembered from the Sundays of his boyhood, he began in a firm, clear voice to preach a sermon.

He was by far the tallest figure on that platform, as well as the one in whom all the folk were absorbed. The black ornat made him seem the taller. The wind that blew the white hair about his face and shook the crisp fluting of the white collar let loose a volley of oak leaves from the neighboring trees, but his voice overrode the wind, and every homely word went straight to the ears of his listeners. They had come from the two parishes, and from beyond Grenaa. In all their lives they were never to hear another sermon like this one, nor one to be remembered longer.

He took the familiar text from the Proverbs, and he began by quoting book and chapter, even as he would have done in his church. "He that is slow to anger is better than the mighty; and he that ruleth his spirit than he that taketh a city." He spoke simply, and for a brief time only, but when he concluded there was no one among them all but believed as never before: the man who restraineth himself from striking his servant is greater than the captain that taketh the King's Copenhagen.

Sören Qvist blessed them, then, his hands held out above them. He knelt thereafter under the hands of Peder Korf, and then took from Villum Ström the white napkin and with it bound his own eyes. He gave a signal to Villum Ström, and the executioner lifted his sword.

Peder Qvist turned away his head. He heard, nonetheless, the whistle of the descending blade, and from the onlookers a great sigh, like the wind in the oak forest, and then a tremendous silence fell upon Aalsö common.

Every step of the way back to Grenaa and beyond, into the dunes, Peder Qvist heard his father's voice, the whistle of the sword, the great sigh of the crowd. Peder had been stationed near to the highroad, and was able to reach it quickly before anyone else had thought of leaving the common. He wished that he had kept the brown horse, and then felt that it was rightly returned to his father's farm. But he could not travel fast enough. Not for anything would he have returned to Aalsö parsonage to speak with Peder Korf, or to Vejlby to see Vibeke in tears. He kept on his way with all the speed he could muster, almost at a trot. Beyond Grenaa the country grew wild. The footpath circled the dunes, and he was not sure where he was going, but by good chance he avoided the branching paths, and early in the afternoon rounded the last dune, came in sight of the hovels on the shore, and, at the water's edge, the boat drawn up and surrounded by a small group of people.

Anna was with them. The fishwife, her man, and the Swedish sailors made up the rest of the gathering. Anna stepped forward to meet her brother, and he caught her by the shoulders and kissed her before he held her from him and, without a word, looked steadily into her clear eyes and nodded, once. Then he said to the men, "How soon can we be gone?"

"We have been ready any minute these last two hours," said the chief of them.

"Then, in God's name, let us be gone. In Denmark, in the year of our Lord 1625, they have beheaded a saint."

His voice was harsh with passion and his face strained; Anna would not have recognized the voice had she not seen the face.

"You cannot leave too quickly for us," said the sailor. "The weather does not grow any kinder. I think we shall have snow by nightfall."